TWO TO TANGO

BY CHARLENE TORKELSON

This book is dedicated to all the dancers I have met, all the dancers I have danced with, and all those I have taught. In some form or another you are a part of this book. A piece of you is in each and every character and in each dance performed. You are a special group of people with unique talents. You have and always will be a part of my life. Since the first year I began ballroom dancing, I have worn a small gold band on my little finger signifying my dedication and connection to all the dancers in the world. This book is for all of you who have played such a significant role in my life. Thank you.

TWO TO TANGO

Introduction:

The car was flattened like an old tin can. Once compact and small, it was now even smaller and certainly more compact. The Minneapolis wind whipped up the dry snow as the long line of waiting cars slowed even more to gawk as they passed – broken glass glittering across the pavement as the hazy sun caught the scattered fragments. The ambulance was long gone and the tow truck was maneuvering in front of the twisted metal to begin the trek to another place.

Just a few miles away, the downtown dance studio was quiet. It was too early for the music to begin and the dance students to meander in for a lesson after work. The usual morning exercise sessions had ceased a few weeks earlier making this morning particularly lonely and bleak around the lower level of the parking ramp where the studio occupied a space. No one was around when the call came in about the accident. The message was simple. There was a car crash, and the driver wasn't expected to survive.

This tale doesn't actually begin today but rather ends here. The occupant of the car was a dancer, or rather a former dancer who discovered it takes two to tango. And that ended several promising careers as well as a life.

I.

Sydney Monroe propped herself onto the corner of the couch in the waiting area of the studio. Bare foot and dressed in a leotard and heavy leg warmers, the heat was beginning to make the space comfortable after an odd morning exercise session. Usually beginning at 9:15 am, she had been the only one attending this morning. The studio owner Edward Garrett was away on dance business and his former wife Amanda who usually partnered with him was also away. The quiet was broken only by the tapping of the computer keys. Receptionist Morgan Canfield was never in before the start of the studio day at 1:00 pm, but today she was completing some of the unfinished business reports from last week. With Edward coming back from his trip today, she calculated the finished reports would sooth some of his wrath. And wrath was what everyone expected whenever Edward was around.

The tinkle of the front door caused Morgan to stop briefly to look up over her reading glasses that had slipped down to the tip of her nose. "May I help you?" she offered.

The young woman who stepped in from the cold was dressed in a thin coat - obviously not a Minnesota native. Her naturally red hair was full and long with large puffy curls. She wore a satiny green dress with matching pumps.

Morgan, sharp tongued and sarcastic, scanned the visitor up and down obviously not approving of her morning attire. "We don't begin lessons until three o'clock …" Morgan began but was cut off in mid sentence by the woman who had not noticed in the least that she was receiving reproving looks from the woman behind the desk.

In a southern drawl, the woman interrupted, "I am looking for my office, if you please." She hastily scanned the desk area and then up and down the sides for office doors. She spotted the door to Edward Garrett's office on the corner of the hallway. His office was reserved only for the privileged few. Most missed it completely because it was closed off with an ornate door, and the floor to ceiling windows that opened out to the dance floor were always heavily curtained to hide the inner sanctuary from the rest of the riff raff. But this woman did not miss it and was heading toward the door with her heavy brocaded fabric bag in tow.

By now Morgan Canfield was quite irritated. Usually a sharp glance from Morgan stopped anyone dead in their tracks, but not today. This woman was clearly out of her mind. She must have turned left when she should have turned right. Morgan was now standing behind the reception desk and pointing. "Stop! Madam, you are in the wrong place. This is a dance studio and not your office," her voice was bellowing.

"Why yes it is," the southern drawl continued as she showed no intention of stopping her intended path. She reached Edward's office door and opened it. "Why this is quite nice. I think I shall be very happy here," she chirped without so much as a glance back at the now red faced Morgan.

As the woman began to heave her tote into the office, Morgan was quickly around the desk and pushing her way in front of the woman barring her way. "Stop!" she ordered so flustered she had nothing more to add. "Stop!" Morgan glared at the woman who was looking at Morgan strangely with a well manicured hand clutching her heart as if in shock at the manners of this woman.

"Well, I never …" the woman sputtered.

"That's right. You never." Morgan was bodily in front of the doorway hands on the frame and legs spread to prevent any further entry. "Who are you?" Morgan demanded.

"Why I'm the new Supervisor, Miss Sheila Pickford," the woman had her nose so high in the air Morgan could see the flare of her nostrils.

Morgan relaxed a bit and said with a smirk, "We have a Supervisor by the name of Suzanna Caldwell who has been in this studio for many years. You are certainly mistaken and must be in the wrong place."

"I don't think so. Edward Garrett hired me specially this weekend. Obviously, you all need help." She emphasized the word "help" and looked down her nose with a glare. "Now, please show me my office."

Morgan pushed her glasses back up her nose and twisted her mouth into a thoughtful purse. She always dressed comfortably and today was in a brown skirt that resembled a sack and a beige sweater with a small scarf around her neck. She wore no makeup and brushed her hand through her mop of dishwater blond hair. Now it was Sheila Pickford's turn to look up and down with disapproval.

"This is Mr. Garrett's private office. You'll have to wait until he arrives …". Once again Sheila Pickford interrupted. "I'll just wait here then." She shoved her way past a startled Morgan into Edward's office and slammed the door.

"We'll see about this one," Morgan muttered and returned to her desk shaking her head. "We'll see ...". Morgan took a deep breath and looked with disgust at the report she was completing.

II.

Edward Garrett usually entered through the back door – the one that opened into the lower level of the parking lot. He only lived a short few blocks away in a spacious condo that overlooked the city skyline. Sometimes he would walk, other times he would pull his big old retro Cadillac into the space reserved for him and take the few steps into the studio through the back door. Today was different. He noisily made his way through the front door with a tall younger man close behind.

"Mr. Garrett…", Morgan Canfield began.

"What is it?" Edward motioned with his hands as if he had no time for anything she could possibly say. He peered over the desk to the spindle that held his messages and blocked out the words of banter that Morgan Canfield was about to spout.

"A Miss Sheila Pickford is waiting in your office. I told her …", but she was cut off with a wave of the hand and a huge grin across the face of the man who resembled Howdy Doody when his curly haired wig was removed. His round freckled face had the cheeks of a chipmunk split in the middle by a dapper mustache and topped by a bowl of curly hair that he continually adjusted whenever he managed to find himself in front of a mirror.

"Lovely!" he chirped. "By the way, this is a new teacher, Daniel Loggerman. Please make a column for him on your schedule." He waved his hand across the large daily schedule of appointments and lessons that took up much of the counter space behind the desk.

"Loggerman?" Morgan Canfield said coldly looking at the tall dark haired man in his early twenties.

Daniel looked embarrassed and nodded. He wore a long wool coat and a smart looking black suit underneath. He carried a neat square black gym bag over his shoulder. Morgan smiled. Edward had gone into his office. The two of them simply looked calmly at each other, and the tension that had cut the air previously was soothed with a quiet gaze.

"Do you teach front department or back?" Morgan calmly asked referring to the two teaching areas of the studio – new student or front department and advanced student or back department.

Daniel smiled. "I was told that I teach front. But I suppose that decision would be up to you." He clearly was a master of smooth, and Morgan Canfield was slowly being sucked in inch by inch by his charm.

"Very well. Front department it is," she smiled back at him and carefully lettered the name at the top of an empty column. "I do hope that I'm spelling Loggerman correctly," she coyly raised an eyebrow.

"Perfect," he flashed a grin that could have melted Antarctica.

Sydney Monroe sat quietly in the corner taking in every bit of drama. She wanted to clear her throat so this Daniel would notice at least her presence, but before she could, the door to Edward Garrett's office flew open. Edward was guiding a giggling Miss Sheila through the door. Her thin coat had been left behind in the office as had her brocade bag. Her shimmering green dress glistened as the morning sunlight flashed through the front window catching each ripple and fold. She tossed back her head of red hair and gazed into Edward's eyes.

This was not an unusual occurrence in the dance studio. Actually, it was all too common. Edward was enthralled with women. It didn't matter if his former wife Amanda was present or not. His attention to other women was a given and had eventually been the downfall of his marriage. Amanda Garrett was probably considered the foremost fashion model in the area. Her picture graced the covers of magazines and newspapers alike. Her tall slender body and classic features were handsome. She was not giggly nor was she cute, but rather a stately beauty that both fascinated and held Edward's attentions in spite of the divorce. He always felt Amanda would understand his dalliances – and she had for a while. Until one of her young model friends – one who had thought of Amanda as a mentor – had caught more than Edward's eye. In spite of the end of the marriage, their relationship had continued. Amanda came into exercise class every morning to keep in shape, and Edward tried in every way possible to win back her affections. They somehow fascinated each other - although no one quite understood why.

Sheila Pickford was not Edward's type. She was not particularly tall and was round and curvy with a flirtatious drawl. But she didn't know she wasn't Edward's ideal woman, and right now she was giving it all she could. Somehow she must have thought the game would give her something. What could that be? Sydney Monroe could only guess. In spite of Edward's wealthy appearance, everyone in the studio knew it was only for show. The studio was always on the edge of financial collapse largely due to Edward's spending sprees. The teachers who worked at this studio were definitely not here for the wealth. Most lived together in apartments on the bus line because no one could afford a car. Every penny they made went right back into costumes and shoes. So whatever

Sheila Pickford imagined she was getting, it certainly wouldn't materialize.

Edward was guiding "the green goddess" around the ballroom and back towards the offices used by Supervisor Suzanna Caldwell, Counselor Antoine Hawks, and the various teachers. The dance floor was airy and open with windows surrounding one wall, floating curtains letting in all the light that the city offered, and of course the glistening hard wood dance floor. In the center was a stone wall that backed the reception desk and acted as a media center island. Speakers, microphones, and of course Edward's collection of drums created a crazy yet distinct texture of sight and sound. It wasn't much of a tour once you left the spacious ballroom. The back offices were marred by old carpet that frequently caught the heels of new dancers unaware of the perils of the back room walks. The old furnace was tucked into the corner giving the back teacher's room a dark ominous feel. Certainly this part of the tour could cause a bit of fright to the currently impressed Miss Sheila Pickford. Sydney expected any moment to hear a screech and a thump from the starry eyed Southern belle as she tumbled from a fall.

Daniel was conversing quietly with Morgan, asking about the city and the bus lines. He asked about housing and room rental. Morgan mentioned she rented a room in a home owned by another teacher's mother. Yes, there was another room for rent in the house. It had just opened up last week as a matter of fact. Talk to Joan Ericson. Her mother owns the house.

Sydney decided he was planning to stay. Where ever he came from, he was planning to stay here. Antoine Hawks entered, took a long look at the new teacher standing in front of the reception desk and tried not to look too excited.

"Antoine Hawks," Morgan motioned toward the door. "Meet our new teacher Daniel Loggerman." Antoine put down his bag and extended a hand toward the new man.

Antoine Hawks was a North Dakota farm boy who came to the big city to find fame and fortune. So far he had found neither. He had changed his non descript given name of Anthony Hawkinson to a more flamboyant Antoine Hawks, cut his hair, and donned more spectacular clothes. He always looked perfect, said the appropriate words, and charmed his way into everyone's heart. It looked as if he had met his match. Sydney pursed her lips and wondered if this was good … or bad.

Sydney wandered past the pair at the front desk to change into appropriate work clothes – always a dress or skirt, pantyhose and dance shoes, and of course, perfect makeup. Although she had danced for years as a teen before coming to the studio, she would never get used to the makeup part of the job. At first, Antoine and Amanda had tried to show her how to apply the cakey mess to her face - the blush on the cheeks, the lipstick and finally the eye shadow and mascara. It was a chore she never enjoyed. "Professional," that's how Edward Garrett had put it. "You must look professional at all times." Today, however, she would sail through the ritual. Today would prove to be a very interesting day, and she couldn't wait to get out to the ballroom for the fireworks that were sure to come.

III.

The ballroom began to fill with teachers pulling out the wrought iron chairs from behind the glass topped circle tables. The tables and chairs normally slid alongside the windows for students as they waited for a group class or practice party to begin were an afterthought during the dance day. Now they were prominently slid across the hardwood floor in preparation for the daily meeting.

Edward Garrett – nicknamed Eddie G behind his back by the staff at the studio – often times conducted the meetings. Sometimes a dynamic speaker full of charisma, other times a raving lunatic who scared a new teacher into submission through pointed criticism and belittling, Edward Garrett was always interesting. He could take you to a point of complete frustration and humiliation then just as quickly lift you higher than you had ever felt before. It was this see saw of emotions that kept the staff always guessing and always willing to do what was expected. It was a unique feeling of always balancing on the edge that kept nerves raw and the mood of the studio always in flux. Today would be no exception.

Edward had wisely kept Miss Sheila Pickford away from the eye of the rest of the staff. Morgan and Sydney were silent, not mentioning anything about her presence.

Sydney found a seat in the corner of the room and watched the procession of staff take their places. Morgan sat behind the reception desk playing with her reading glasses and shaking her head in anticipation of the fireworks that would soon take place. She kept her head down as teachers passed the desk and checked the daily schedule. It was not her place to begin the fire – only to watch it sizzle.

The "head table" was moved to the center of the floor, and Antoine Hawks took his seat as front department Counselor. Supervisor Suzanna Caldwell quietly put her armload of paperwork down on the table on the other end so Edward Garrett would be in the middle between them. Suzanna was perhaps the most admired dancer in the group. To look at this tiny, almost birdlike woman with the big round glasses and mousey bobbed hair as a great dancer would be almost unthinkable at first glance. She was not glamorous nor was she the handsome featured model that Amanda Garrett was. She looked rather like a maiden aunt. But she knew more about dance technique and teaching than anyone in the room - including the creative and nationally admired Eddie G. Although Edward did not like to give her credit for the talent she had worked so hard to develop, she knew he was also an admiring fan although it was way deep down in his inner most being where that admiration was buried. And he would not let it surface under any circumstances for the rest of the world to see. Suzanna was a patient woman and waited for the day when Edward Garrett would say those three little words she longed to hear – "You are great!"

As always, the group waited. Edward Garrett was tucked away in his office with the curtains drawn. There was the saying in the studio "You have real time and you have Garrett time." In other words, Eddie G was never on time for anything. If there was an event that needed his presence at the real time, the rest of the staff was careful to tell him the start was at least two hours before it actually was. That way it might get him there on time – or it might just make him only an hour late.

Edward Garrett angled his way past the front desk with long lanky strides, patted his hair and ushered in his smiling new addition to the staff. He pulled a chair from the nearest table and promptly placed her between his chair and Suzanna Caldwell. People stared and watched as Suzanna continued to look straight ahead not a nod to her side nor an acknowledgement of the woman seated next to her. It was as if she was psychic and knew just what was about to happen.

"Let me introduce our two new staff additions," he began with a sweep of his arm. "Miss Sheila Pickford ...". Sheila rose from her seat and flashed a smile in Edward's direction. "And Mr. Daniel Loggerman." Daniel stood, nodded his head and quickly sat down again. "They will be joining our team. As you all know I was in Kansas City this weekend and worked with various studio teams. Clearly these two showed talents that we can use here in Minneapolis."

"In other words, they were thinking of quitting at their other studio due to personality conflicts..." Carson Hunter whispered to Sydney. Sydney managed to control her impulse to laugh and gazed at Suzanna. Suzanna had placed a tiny hand across her mouth and continued to stare straight ahead.

Edward rambled on for a few more minutes talking about the extraordinary impact his presence at the training seminar has been then dropped the bomb shell that Morgan Canfield had been waiting for. "Mr. Loggerman will be teaching in our front department and Miss Pickford will be our Supervisor." Morgan peaked around the corner of the desk to check out the reactions.

Suzanna Caldwell didn't change her expression nor her stare. Antoine Hawks gasped noticeably and cocked

17

his head to take a better look at Sheila Pickford. Sheila herself was preparing to make a speech of acceptance however Edward continued to go on and on about the greatness of the studio and tremendous impact all of the talent in this room would make on the dance world. He clearly was trying to move past the sentence he had just spoken to other more cheerful matters. Anna Smith was not taken in. She politely raised her hand and waited. Edward ignored her for a few moments until each and every hand in the room – except of course those at the front table – were raised. Daniel Loggerman raised his hand along with the rest as a show of unity Sydney supposed.

Edward sputtered. "Yes, Miss Smith. What is the problem?"

"Excuse me for pointing this out, but we already have a Supervisor." She motioned to Miss Caldwell.

"Yes, but I have promoted Miss Caldwell to Manager," Edward announced.

Sheila Pickford's face changed dramatically from a smiling Miss America waving star to a bitter seething wench.

Miss Smith once again raised her hand.

"Yes, what is it?" Edward was becoming impatient with her persistence.

"But, Miss Caldwell is already our manager." Anna Smith's voice became just as impatient as Edward Garrett's.

Everything went downhill from there. Morgan Canfield sat back and watched as words flew back and forth between the staff and Edward. His attitude of course was that it was **his** studio and **he** made the decisions and this decision was what was best for the studio. Eventually, Edward stomped off to his office and slammed the door. Sheila Pickford left for lunch without her thin little coat and with a scowl on her face that gave Morgan tremendous pleasure. The staff bustled around the studio like a swarm of bees, and Daniel Loggerman was wondering why he had decided to ever come to Minneapolis.

Daniel did eventually have a chance to sit down with Joan Ericson to discuss the apartment available in her mother's home. Edward Garrett cooled down and called Suzanna Caldwell into his office for a discussion that lasted well into the evening. In fact the door to his office remained closed after the last of the staff left for the night.

IV.

Sydney managed to get to the studio as usual before anyone else. "Why do I even bother to go to this morning exercise class?" she asked herself as she leaned against the concrete blocked wall. "No one else on the staff except Antoine even bothers to come in for these sessions. What exactly do I expect to gain from this torture?" She sorted out her feelings. It kept her in great shape to go through the exercises each morning. She had this vision of herself actually dancing as a star, not just a teacher in a studio. Although she looked younger than her 28 years, age was creeping up. It was a now or never attitude that drove her to take advantage of any additional training that was offered. She secretly thought she might have a chance to become Edward's next dance partner. He wasn't the easiest person to dance with – all of his creativity was eventually lost when he routinely forgot the patterns he had choreographed himself right in the middle of a performance. She had heard the stories from Anna Smith over and over. Anna had danced several times with Edward before Amanda Garrett had finally consented to become his dance partner after their break up. Anna said the experience was dreadful. First, you learn a complicated routine then Edward changes it during the performance

20

making all that practice worthless. It was a humiliating experience. Sydney kept her dream inside never sharing it with any of the other staff.

"Hey," Antoine Hawks waltzed in. "Isn't anyone here yet?" Sydney picked up her duffle bag and shook her head.

"I'll let you in and then I really need a little coffee this morning. I'll be right back." He opened the door and relocked it behind her.

Sydney didn't bother with the lights. There was a security light that shone in the reception area. So she dragged her bag back to the teachers' office to store. It took her a few minutes to doff her shoes and coat. She let out a frustrated exhale and closed her eyes for a moment. Forcing herself to get up off the chair, she slowly meandered down the hallway hoping no one was out on the floor yet.

Edward's door was open. His voice boomed causing her to stop and press herself against the wall. "You owe me a partner!" he bellowed.

Amanda's voice echoed back, "I have been a partner and a good one at that. I'm a model not a dancer. This opportunity is too good a chance for me to pass up so stop being so selfish."

"Selfish? You call me selfish? What do you think you are doing leaving me high and dry when I have some of my best dance opportunities coming up." Edward was furious.

"You are the one who cheated on me. And with one of my friends – a fellow model who was under aged I might add. Who exactly was selfish there?"

"I shipped her off to another studio when you found out didn't I?"

"Well, goodie for you. Too bad she had a nervous breakdown before she even reached 18. When do you ever think about anything or anyone with your brain instead of your you-know-what? I don't owe you anything." Amanda Garrett was quiet for a moment, and Edward had no verbal response. He was probably sulking. He sulked very well. Sydney could just imagine him sitting in his big overstuffed office chair while Amanda stood, his head down and his lower lip jetting out. Just like a small boy.

"Ok. I'll make you a deal," Amanda finally broke the silence. "I'll find you a dance partner. Someone good."

"You know when I mean good I don't just mean a smooth dancer. She has to look the part – tall and thin. You know. A media star. Someone the cameras will be drawn to." Edward, the almost 40 year old dancer, wanted glitz and glamour. Sydney pressed back into the wall even more tightly. Obviously, he didn't mean her. End of dream.

The next morning Amanda had brought in a "friend" – another model for the exercise class. Kerri Blake was stunning. She was tall like Amanda but unlike Amanda's thin boyish figure, Kerri was all legs and more angular. She unknotted her long blond hair and retied it into a cascade of unruly tresses. Her smile was alluring – uneven yet real somehow. Edward immediately tried to make a good impression by showing his good side. The entire session he smiled and grinned at everyone. This was not only new and different – it was a first never to be repeated.

Kerri took a spot next to Amanda in the front row. Sydney and Antoine were behind in the second row. "Don't worry, you'll get the step," Edward purred whenever Kerri stopped to contemplate a move. Kerri was pleasant. Sydney had to admit she actually did like Kerri. It did seem to drag her mood down a bit to realize that this person might be edging into a partnership dance role simply because she had longer legs. That seemed to be the truth of the matter. What else could she think?

Sydney watched as Edward invited both Amanda and Kerri into his private office to use as their changing room at the end of the exercises. Never had Sydney been invited inside the door to that office. It was a message that sang loud and clear to her. But then would she want that invitation? Probably not. Kerri was too young to realize that she was walking into the spider's web. And the web didn't let anyone go without a fight. Just look at Amanda taking the blame for Edward's affair. She would never escape no matter how hard she fought.

Sydney changed for lessons and leaned on the front desk staring at her daily appointments. "What's the matter?" Morgan snapped as Sydney seamed lost in thought.

"Nothing really." Sydney stood to the side and felt her body sink. Morgan didn't give up so easily and pressed a little more until the front door opened and Sheila Pickford stomped in.

"I'm going to kill him!" She muttered under her breath as she shook out her still too thin coat flecked with wisps of snowflakes.

"Who? Who are you going to kill? Mr. Garrett?" Morgan had a new person to banter with.

"What? No. Daniel Loggerman is the worst human being in the entire world. And that's a fact!" She began to tighten her fists. "We are unfortunately roommates. He is a total slob." She began to count off on her fingers. "He never comes home at night. And he didn't bother to give me the rent today when he knew it was due. So now I'm stuck paying the whole thing until he remembers to give me the money. Which may be never."

Morgan frowned. Her initial impression of Sheila had not been very good. It remained on the shaky side even after the public humiliation she suffered that took her down a peg. But Daniel. She had loved Daniel, and this complaining from someone who was not a favorite clearly did not sit well.

"You must be mistaken." Morgan didn't really go all out to defend Daniel, but she was not going to let these comments go unanswered.

"You live there." Sheila stared back at Morgan. "Do you see him coming home at night? Have you come upstairs to check on the condition the apartment is in? Would you forget to pay the rent and let someone else shoulder this financial burden?" Her drawl twanged unmercifully.

"Well..." Morgan was speechless.

"I am furious!" And with that Sheila stomped off to the back office. Her little dream office had turned into the big dark boiler room that she shared with "the manager", "the counselor", and all the other teachers.

Kerri was coming out of Edward's office followed by Mr. Garrett himself. He steered her to the front desk and once again pointed to the schedule. "Miss Canfield, please make a column for Miss Blake. She will be a new teacher slash specialist." He gave her one of his big grins.

"Hi, I'm Kerri Blake," the lanky model extended her hand across the desk to a gaping Miss Canfield.

Morgan picked up a marker and starred. "Blake you say? B-L-A-K-E?"

"Exactly. I'm looking forward to spending some time here in the studio." She looked over at Sydney who slumped even more into the top of the desk. Then she turned to follow Edward back into his office.

"What is going on around here?" Morgan glanced curiously at Sydney but Sydney only shrugged and scurried out to the dance floor.

V.

Several weeks passed and the mood in the studio mellowed. Suzanna and Sheila didn't become "friends" exactly, but there was an air of tolerance. Suzanna simply waited for Sheila to make mistakes. And her inexperience certainly brought out mistakes. Kerri Blake seemed to show up every morning for exercise class with more and more confidence. Eddie G. was choreographing a new jazzy routine to a smooth and mellow Motown tune that had just hit the charts. The routine was different – it wasn't really a partner routine, but rather a threesome. He, Amanda, and Kerri were the three dancers. Sydney simply followed behind picking up here and there the movements Edward was concocting. It just made her more determined to become one of the show dancers. No matter what it took, she would never give up.

It was one gloomy almost spring day when Sydney dragged in for class in a particularly foul mood. She had taken her bag to the back teachers' office and had nearly tripped over a lump of green fluff. It turned out after she flipped the light switch that right in the middle of the room was a puffed up dance dress in bright emerald green.

"This must be the monstrosity that Sheila Pickford has been droning on and on about," Sydney muttered.

27

Sheila had chatting incessantly about a ballroom dance dress she owned. Edward was one who had no use for the fluffy dance dresses that were currently popular in the ballroom world. Instead he dressed his dancers in sleek disco attire with form fitting lines and lots of glitz and glamour. This dress on the floor was clearly outrageous. It had layers and layers of stiff skirts and a sagging top that drooped into the circled waist created by the layers of fabric. Sydney leaped over the blob reaching her desk to change clothes. This would be a major joke when the rest of the staff saw the dress. It would be the laugh that kept the staff sane for the next few weeks. She simply shook her head and leaped back over to get to the door.

The ballroom was dark. Edward was seated on the floor alone. He had begun to stretch and had his capped head bouncing furiously toward his toes. Edward never wore his toupee when exercising, so wore a small knit cap to hide his bald head. It was forever frustrating for him that the other dancers – mostly women – were more flexible than he was. So it made him push even harder and more violently to stretch his stiff old legs.

He didn't speak as Sydney hit the floor to follow his movement. They exercised in silence for several minutes before Edward rose and finally put on a piece of music. It was a Tango. Sultry and dark, the tango was a dance from Argentina depicting the love and hate conflict between men and women. This particular Tango was typical. It moved between a fast and lively section into a slow rich romantic few bars.

"The Tango tells a story," Edward began as he put the music on for a second time. "It tells the story of a man and a woman who vacillate between loving each other and hating each other." He didn't look at Sydney but rather kept his gaze toward the stone wall that held the sound equipment. Continuing he explained, "The woman is trying her best to please the man, but he pushes her away punishing her for not showing total attention to him. She grovels and pleads for forgiveness, and he finally relents allowing her to move back into his graces."

Sydney pondered these words. She knew the story of the Tango and this seemed to be a bit of an exaggeration. Yes, it was a story of love and hate, but the groveling and the punishment didn't seem to fit into her interpretation. "Ok," she nodded.

"I have a new routine in mind. Something that should really tell the story, and I would like you to partner this Tango with me." He still did not turn to look at her.

"Ok," she hesitated. This was what she had dreamed of - a dance partnership that could springboard her dance career. Somehow this seemed wrong. It didn't sound the way she had imagined it would.

"I need your total and complete cooperation to make this Tango believable," Edward swung around to face her and stared directly into her eyes. The intensity was sudden and shocking.

Sydney simply nodded and moved to face him out on the dance floor. "I am going to slap you. You fall to the floor cowering in fear, then slink toward me on your belly begging for forgiveness." He stood defiantly with a scowl on his face as he explained the choreography. "Then you crawl up my leg – begging, meekly sorrowful for your inattention – I look at you, then pull you up to me …".

Edward was never able to finish his sentence. Sydney burst into laughter. She was laughing so hard she had to turn away.

"Don't you dare walk away from me," he bellowed as she began to walk off the dance floor. "You'll never get a chance like this again," he sputtered.

Sydney simply walked back into the back room, grabbed her bag and continued out the front door. She sat in the coffee shop next door nursing a cup of coffee and debating what to do next. Today would be no problem. She would wait until other staff members arrived. Edward would never say anything about the incident with others around. But what about tomorrow's exercise class? How could she handle another possible one on one exercise session? Then and there, she decided not to go back in the mornings. She would become another staff member who didn't go to the morning exercise class. Maybe the others had already experienced what she had today. Maybe they just never shared that experience with her. Her dream was indeed dead.

It was a week before Edward finally confronted Sydney. She had managed to avoid him in the studio during working hours. It really wasn't that difficult. He rarely came out of his office when he was even in the studio. But it was that Friday when she began to walk down the hall to the teachers' office at the end of the evening when he stepped out of his office directly in her path. "Why aren't you coming into exercise in the mornings?" he asked without so much as a mention of the Tango incident. It was as if he had no idea what he had done, what he had said, what he had shown her about his mood and attitude toward women.

Sydney hesitated to answer not wanting to look him directly in the eyes. "Come into my office a minute," he stepped aside to usher her in.

There was no other place to go. She could not get around him, and she didn't feel like turning around and bolting out the front door. She decided then and there as she walked through the doorway. She could either be timid and let him control the situation or she could be aggressive and on the offensive. She chose the latter. Taking a deep breath and pressing her dry lips together firmly, she entered the forbidden chambers.

He sat down in his large padded leather chair with her standing in front of his desk just as he had with Amanda during their argument. It put him in control. But this time, Sydney took charge and began to speak. It was unexpected to him that she would have such nerve. She leaned forward, hands on top of the dark cherry desk, and looked into his eyes.

"You ask why I am not coming in to exercise class? You clearly have chosen a new dance partner. Yet I have been coming in, working out, and training very hard for months. Why did you choose Kerri over me? Is she a better dancer than I am?" She waited for him to shake his head "no". There was nothing more than a no that he could answer – it was a loaded question. Obviously Sydney had much more dance experience than Kerri. Sydney continued in a sing songy voice. "Is she prettier than I am?" Again he had to shake "no". The question put him in a spot with no place to go. He couldn't very well say Kerri was prettier. He would have to defend a yes, and he was unable to at this point. "It's because you're fucking her." This was a statement and not a question.

Edward Garrett was so taken back, he nearly fell backwards in his chair. The shocked look on his face was worth the fear Sydney experienced in saying the words.

After a moment of silence, Edward gained a bit of composure and spoke. "I feel like Christ, and you are nailing me to the cross." He made some sounds with his mouth. "Fump. Fump." Then whipped his arms back into side positions and dropped his head into a hang dog death drop with his tongue dragging from his mouth. "I didn't know you had it in you to say those words to me. You just crucified me. I respect you and your position. I respect your guts for saying that to me. Why don't you come back to class tomorrow morning, and we'll start over again. You have a valid complaint." He smiled and that was it. It was over.

Sydney left the room with her only thoughts disgust at the sacrilege. He compared himself to Christ. How did he dare think he could be in the same sentence as a crucified Christ? She relished the horror his face had shown when she said her piece, yet in the same moment he had declared himself a saint for listening to it. How could that have happened? Twisted.

The next morning was dark and drizzly. The chilly rain and whipping winds made visibility from the bus stop almost impossible. Sydney wore her long billowing khaki rain coat with hood to shield herself somewhat from the drops. With each step forward, she found herself dragged back another step. Downtown on a Saturday morning was desolate and empty especially in this weather. She fought her way toward the studio all the while wondering why she had even ventured out. Crossing the street in mid block right in front of the parking lot, her hood covered her face as she plunged forward. Struggling to get up on the curb, she hit something. It wasn't simply a bottle or piece of trash. It was big. Big enough that she had to step over it like she had with Sheila's green ball gown. Turning behind her to see what had stopped her progress, she saw a large pile of clothing and a person. It was probably a street person who had fallen. She reached down to touch him and pull back the coat that had blown over his face. "Oh, my God!" She flinched. It was Edward Garrett. She tried to shake him – wake him up. When that seemed futile, she ran inside the building for help.

Joan Ericson was at the desk doing the week's end paperwork. Sydney explained what had just happened. Joan looked concerned but said as she was picking up the phone to call for help, "Many times over the past few years I've had to help Mr. Garrett into the studio from that very curb. He used to drink heavily you know. But he's been dry for a year or two." She shook her head. "I can't believe he's begun to drink again. That would be disturbing."

They both waited at the door peering through the rain for the ambulance. The flash of red in the distance was quick. But when it stopped and the two ran out to talk with the paramedics, they heard the shocking news. Edward Garrett was not drunk, nor was he injured from falling. He was in fact dead!

VI.

Joan Ericson, Morgan, and Suzanna huddled behind the front desk comforting each other. It wasn't that they were heartbroken over the loss but rather shocked at the circumstances. Joan was shaking her head and reminding Suzanna how many times they had both helped a drunken Edward Garrett into the studio after a night of drinking.

"He was such a strange one," Joan was saying. "He never slept. Just drank and partied all night and on into the day. It was his fear of getting old that finally made him stop. Aging was his biggest fear." She shook her head and Suzanna nodded in agreement. Morgan, newer to the studio, grimaced. "Why did you ever stay? It's disgusting as it is with him sober. I can't imagine what it would be like with him knock down drunk."

Suzanna, thick glasses hiding a small tear that was forming, tried to explain. "It was the dance. Or rather the love of dance. No matter what anyone said about Edward, he instilled a love of dance in everyone he met. I don't quite know how he did it. He was such a hateable person. Is that a word? He had such strange moods and habits that really were so irritating, yet he made you love the movement, the music, and the whole world of dance." Joan nodded in agreement. "I don't like to think of him out

36

there in the rain lying in the gutter dead. It just doesn't seem right. He wasn't that old. It's hard to talk about him in the past rather than the present."

Sydney sat in the corner listening and cradling her head in her arms. She knew everyone was assuming Edward died from drinking or a fall. Somehow in her gut she knew he had died a more violent death and one that wasn't natural. She hadn't looked closely when she pulled back the coat, but there was something that wasn't right about his appearance other than being very dead. She had never seen a dead person before. It was a very unpleasant experience. The whole morning was unpleasant. The rain, the wind, the darkness, and the body. She wondered if anyone had heard the conversation she had with Edward the night before. That would not be good. The one time she had shown some backbone, and the person she directs her anger toward dies. Not good. She shook her wet hair trying to somehow feel warmer but the chill remained.

Amanda and Kerri were outside talking with police. They had come together late for exercise and had watched the yellow police tape cord off the small part of the street in front of the studio. Amanda's face looked pale as she tried to keep a professional expression. Kerri was putting her arm around her shoulder to give more support as the conversation continued.

"This is going to be a sad day," Joan was saying as she gazed out the window trying to determine how Amanda was taking the news. "She seems to be surprised but not overly shocked." She pointed to Amanda slowly nodding her head to the words the policeman was saying. The policeman guided Amanda and Kerri into a squad car and drove away.

Joan was pulling back the thin curtains from the window. "Probably needs someone to identify the body. That would be my guess."

Sheila Pickford dragged herself in the front door. She hadn't noticed the yellow tape nor anything else that was going on out on the sidewalk. Head down with a closed umbrella dragging behind her, the clomp clomp of her shoes was accented by the click clicking of the tip of the umbrella on the cement. She frowned as she opened the door and stared at the four women pressed to the front window. "Humph!" She grunted and turned to drag the umbrella down the hall to the office.

A detective came into the studio and looked around. "Could you direct me to the person who discovered the body, please?" He pulled out a notebook and tapped his pen.

Heads turned toward Sydney. "That would be me," she piped up with a twist of her lips and a scrunched up face.

"Could we talk a moment?" he motioned toward the tables in the ballroom. She nodded and headed as far back as possible.

Slowly she related how she was coming to the studio for an exercise class. She described how difficult it was to walk with the storm and heavy rain, how she had crossed the street and tripped over the body in the gutter. "I'm sure someone will tell you that Edward and I had a bit of an argument last night..." she decided truth at the start was the best approach.

The officer raised an eyebrow and let her continue. "I'm not one to fight with people verbally, or physically for that matter," she added the last part when she realized how it must have sounded. "But he wanted to know why I wasn't coming into morning practices, so I decided to be honest and tell him."

"And exactly why was that?" the officer prompted.

"I have been working hard to really get some place with my dancing, and Edward brought in a new inexperienced dancer to become his new partner. I didn't feel that was fair, and I told him so." Sydney swallowed hard. "He actually took it much better than I expected. He invited me to come back to practices. Which is why I was here early this morning. For practice."

"I see. What is your relationship to the deceased?"

"No relationship. Boss, employee. Dancer, dancer. If you are asking if I was involved with Edward... no, definitely not. I'm not really his type."

"What is his type?" the officer stared at her face.

"You know. Like Amanda, his ex-wife and Kerri, the woman who was out on the curb with Amanda. They are models if you couldn't tell just from looking. He likes them tall and thin." Then as if to prove her point, she stood up. "See, short and average."

"Did that make you angry? I mean did you want him to be attracted to you?" the officer frowned.

"Oh, no. Not at all. I think anyone who was involved with Edward would be crazy. Personally, I found him to be, well, unattractive as a personality. He wasn't a person I found very likeable. No. Not at all." Sydney tried to explain without saying something derogatory about the dead. He would find out soon enough what Edward Garrett was like.

"So who was involved with him?"

"Well, I wouldn't be the one to ask. I'm not that close that I would know much about his personal life. But I'm sure Amanda – his wife – would be able to tell you more."

The officer thanked her and rose to go back toward the desk. The three women, Suzanna, Morgan, and Joan were crowded together trying their hardest to listen to the conversation, but only picked up bits and pieces.

"Do you know anyone who would want to hurt or kill Edward Garrett?" the officer's question stunned them only for a second before Joan blurted out, "Who wouldn't? That would be a better question."

The officer smiled and thanked them for their time.

"Excuse me officer," Joan started. He turned around. "Are you suggesting that Edward Garrett's death wasn't an accident or a natural death?"

"At this point we don't actually know what the cause of death was. We will have to wait for an autopsy report. But I can say this. He didn't appear to die naturally. A fall maybe or something else. So we will be looking into all possibilities as we wait for the report. Ladies?" He nodded his head and turned to leave.

"Hmmm. I hadn't thought about it being anything other than a drunken fall." Joan and Suzanna looked at each other - their minds busily going over the names of those who might become suspects.

At that same moment, Sydney was carefully going over the details of the previous evening. Had she noticed anything out of the ordinary? Would she be someone who they might suspect of harming Edward? How exactly had he died? She needed to know.

There would be a time to come when the entire staff would be interviewed and the very question that officer had asked would be a central issue. Who would want to harm or kill Edward Garrett?

Sheila clumped her way to the front desk. "What are you doing here on a Saturday?" Morgan asked. "How did you hear so quickly about Edward?"

Sheila seemed to be in her own little world. "I have paperwork that didn't get finished … what did I hear about Edward? I haven't heard anything about Edward."

"He's dead," Morgan's deadpan expression remained solemn.

"Great! Does that mean I don't have to suffer with this paperwork? Does this mean I can go home and get some sleep? Does this mean I don't have to go through any more of his God forsaken meetings?" Sheila turned and clumped toward the teachers' office.

"Really. I'm not kidding. He's really dead," Morgan called after her frowning at the response she received.

"Good!"

The day continued in its gloomy darkness. The rain periodically crashed against the large bay windows then just as quickly stopping to a cold foggy calm. Then again the winds would begin again and rain torrents pelted the empty streets.

Amanda Garrett after identifying the body was seated across from a detective far away from the driving rains and chilling winds. She remained unemotional and calm - the events of the day not yet settling in. Amanda's chiseled features were neither cute nor soft. She had the look of a Greek goddess – long narrow nose, thin lipped, large dark eyes and a mass of curled dark hair piled on top of her head by a clip that let the loose ends fall softly around her face and neck. She wore no makeup today and her oversized sweatshirt was cut away at the neck and bottom. Beneath she wore layers. First a t-shirt covering a plain black leotard, then sweat pants over pale pink ballet tights that had been cut with a scissors to rid her feet of the heels and toes. Her bag overflowed with leg warmers, headbands, and big wool socks.

"I'm sorry for your loss, Mrs. Garrett," the detective began.

"I'm officially the ex- Mrs. Garrett," Amanda corrected. "We've been divorced for about nine months now. We had been married about five years."

"And might I ask what the cause of the break up was?"

"Edward always had an eye for other women. I knew that when we married. Maybe that is what attracted me to him in the first place. He had a charisma that drew me to him. But it also drew others to him as well. I found a young model who was from a difficult home situation – no father and the mother needing financial help. I brought her to the studio, and she began to teach part time as well as dance for shows with Edward. The money was good and she was a beautiful dancer – really a nice partner for him. She was only seventeen so we tried to help her out as best we could, considering the situation her mother was in. I travel occasionally to model ... mostly to New York for some of the runway shows. At my age, I try to take all the opportunities I can. After all, modeling is a profession dominated by the young. I'm not exactly old, but for this business I am on the edge. I left to do a show one week and when I came home early, discovered the two of them were having an affair. I could hardly be angry with Elenor. She was so young and vulnerable. But Edward. He not only cheated on me but he cheated a young girl. That was unforgivable. I packed up my things and moved out right then and there. Edward wanted desperately to get back together. He sent Elenor to a studio in another state. It was the largest studio in the country and looked on the outside to be a great opportunity for her, but I knew the truth about the situation. She had a break down a few weeks later. She had to be institutionalized and is struggling to regain her own life back at this point. I've had to take on the roll of dance partner until someone else is found."

"Are you a dancer then?"

"I have come in to the fitness classes for years now to help me stay in shape for my modeling career. I even tried to help out with the studio when we were first married but soon realized that I wasn't really cut out for that kind of thing. I do love to dance, and I don't think I do it too badly if I do say so myself. But, no I am not really a 'dancer'. My life is slowly growing apart from Edward and his dance world. I'm rather glad about that in a way. It is very hard work. And we do fight when we practice. He wants to dominate – show he knows it all. I think I should have a little input as well. I do have experience in what looks good. I have an opinion, too." Amanda talked easily. Normally very congenial and interested in others, she was not really such a chatter box. But today, the shock had opened up her need to talk it all out.

"With Edward's death, do you inherit the studio or any substantial amount of money?" the detective asked.

"Follow the money," Amanda laughed. "I was raised in a very upper class family. I'm a spoiled little rich girl to some, I suppose. I attended a private school and basically was given everything I could ever want or need. Which is why I don't really need as much as others want. I live quite comfortably and plainly I might add, in a little four-plex apartment near the downtown area. It's not even in a very nice neighborhood, but it's artsy and quaint. I have a one bedroom and try not to drive too often. I usually take the bus to where ever I'm going. It suits me. Edward may appear to have money with the studio and all, but I don't think he really has anything to give to anyone. He is quite broke. He spends as fast as he earns. He has expensive tastes unfortunately. So I'm sure he owes more than he has at this point."

"Do you know much about the studio? I mean who he is close to? Has he had any problems or arguments with any of the staff? That kind of thing."

"I only hear rumors. Two of the other apartments in my building are rented by studio staff members, so I hear about things through the grapevine. But they would have more knowledge of what is happening there, I'm afraid. Why do you want to know about that? Enemies?"

"I'm sorry to have to tell you this, but Edward Garrett did not die naturally. We think he was murdered."

Amanda drew back showing for the first time emotion. "Oh my God," she muttered shaking her head and wiping a tear from her cheek.

"Might I ask the full name of the young girl you told me about as well as the two staff members in your building?" The detective tapped his notebook pad.

"Certainly. I don't know where you might find Elenor. Her name is Elenor Reece. Her mother lives here in town I believe, but I don't know if she is back here or not. Antoine Hawks lives on one side of me. We are both on the second floor, and Suzanna Caldwell lives below me." She hesitated. "How do you think he was killed?"

"We think possibly a blow to the head and then he may have been run over."

47

"With a car? Run over with a car? Well that would limit your suspects then. Very few of the people in the studio drive. Most ride the bus. Hmmm." Amanda pondered this last development.

"Quite possibly he was hit by someone other than the person who murdered him," the detective offered. "That would bring that list of suspects up again, I imagine." He snapped his notebook closed and rose. "Do you need a ride back to the studio?"

VII.

Amanda curled up on her sofa hugging a satin pillow. The apartment building in which she lived was a two story older stone structure with quaint windows, dormers and a cement stoop for an entrance. The sides of the building were nicely vine covered. Her own apartment was old fashioned with contemporary furnishings. The nooks and crannies were sparsely filled with a low backed khaki sofa and several large pillows in burnt orange and celery green along with glass and chrome book shelves and coffee tables. Amanda had shared Edward's enthusiasm for art, but her taste was very contemporary rather than the primitive Caribbean that he preferred. Her walls had several large paintings splashed with color. One wall had an array of black and white photos of Amanda. It wasn't anything egotistical, but rather art – poses that made you want to stare at the shadows and lines of the composition without noticing it was anyone in particular.

The rain had stopped and the evening was beginning to feel humid and even a bit warm. Amanda could hear voices coming down the street. Antoine and several friends had gone dancing at a local club. She could hear his laugh as they got to the outside stoop.

She stood at the top of the stairs to wait. Antoine had been a good friend. Not only because he lived so close, but they seemed to have an emotional connection that went a step beyond friendship. He had helped her through the divorce and would certainly get her through this situation as well.

"Hey," he called out when he saw her standing at the door. His friends slid by him and entered his apartment. "How did it go?" he asked.

"It was hard to see him that way. Dead. They think he was murdered." He drew closer. Antoine was wearing crinkled silk pants that ballooned down to a fitted ankle, a white sleeveless tank, and a brightly colored blue rain slicker. He had on a white baseball cap hiding his short spiky hair. His hair was constantly changing. He wanted to remain professional in appearance, yet still on the cutting edge of fashion. Today it was short. A few weeks ago it had been longer and curly.

"Are you a suspect?" he asked.

"Of course I'm a suspect. I'm the ex-wife." Her thin lips pressed together.

"Do you need me to stay with you for a while?" his voice coddled as if speaking to a small child.

"No. I'm fine, and you have friends over."
Amanda returned to her very much in control aloof self.
"Be prepared for the police to interview you, too. You live
near me and might have some information, you know. Ex-
wife … time of death. All that sort of thing." She bit her
lip ever so slightly and knew she could count on her
friendship with Antoine to give her an alibi once they
determined when Edward was killed. He would stand by
her she was sure.

VIII.

Suzanna wasn't surprised by the knock on her door. Once the news that Edward was murdered found its way quickly along the studio grapevine, she knew she would be interviewed. Surely someone would have mentioned her recent replacement as Supervisor. That would send up a red flag quickly.

She let the detective in and offered him a seat. Her apartment below Amanda's was quite different in appearance and feel. It still had the old fashioned nooks, but these were filled with small antique end tables, tea cups and doilies. Her sofa was big and overstuffed. It had taken an army to get it into the apartment originally. Luckily she was on the first floor. The patterned sofa was covered with a throw blanket knit by her grandmother. Her tiny terrier was yapping at her feet until she sat down and picked him up to sit in her lap. "There, there," she calmed him at the presence of a stranger.

"I understand Edward was murdered …", she began getting right to the point.

"Not very surprising."

"Really? Why do you say that?" The officer clicked his pen.

"Edward was the kind of person everyone loved to hate. And he really didn't mind that. It gave him control – a power over everyone else's feelings and moods. He could quickly take you from being a happy person to being downright miserable in an instant. It was something he could do very well."

"And you? Did you hate him too?"

"I'm sure you heard about a situation recently. I had been the Supervisor at the studio, and he hired a new woman to take my place. I remained the studio's manager, but the change cost me quite a bit financially. You see we are paid on a commission basis and when I held both titles, I received a double commission. Now my income has been cut in half. That isn't too pleasant." Suzanna gripped her dog a little tighter causing him to yelp.

"Did that make you angry?"

"Angry enough to kill him? No. I've gone through this same situation many times before. It was no different. Difficult, but not different. Edward has a tendency to move in a young pretty thing in hopes that he will have some kind of relationship with her. I'm not that young, and not that pretty." Suzanna smiled. It was true she was a tiny older woman with years of experience. The kind you could always depend on, but not the kind you would try to seduce. She was too worldly, too wise, and too self sufficient to intimidate. It worked in her favor most of the time except when she had to endure a change such as this one with Sheila Pickford. Miss Pickford would not remain in the studio for long. That was one thing Suzanna could always count on. They never did. "I'm not too worried. Things will change back as they always do. Except, I almost forgot, Edward is dead. That might cause a change that I never anticipated." She began to frown and ponder for a moment. "No, I don't really know what exactly I should expect in this situation."

"What can you tell me about Elenor Reece?"

"Elenor? She was one of Edward's young things. She's gone and will never come back I'm sure. He pretty much destroyed her. So young she was, too. Such a shame." Suzanna shook her head. "I can't give you the details like someone else could. I imagine Amanda would know far more than I do about that situation and about Elenor herself. I've heard rumors. Rumors, rumors, rumors. The studio is basically about rumors. Never anything direct – just what someone else might say that leads you to your own conclusions. In ten or twenty years, we'll get together for a staff reunion, and Elenor Reece will show up and tell us all about what a wonderful life she has now. I imagine that's how it will work out." Suzanna had been through this too many times in the past to think things would change. She was the rock, the anchor. Alone and growing older, she would live in a life unchanged year after year. She and her little dog.

"Thank you Miss Caldwell. If you think of anything that might help us with our investigation, please let us know. Oh, by the way, do you know who locked up on Friday night? Who was the last one in the studio?" He reopened his notebook and waited poised for her answer.

Suzanna frowned. "Normally it would be Joan. She stays until everyone is gone, but I do believe Edward may have been in his office when she left. We both were about to leave around the same time that evening. The door would have been locked. We wouldn't have left him in the studio alone with the door unlocked. It wasn't something we normally did. You can never tell with Edward. He may not remember to check the locks before leaving you know. Normally he left by the back door. That was something that seemed strange to me on Saturday morning after the accident. Why was he out in the front of the building? It wasn't normal for him to leave that way."

"Thank you. That observation might help us out very much." He nodded his head and left.

IX.

Sydney Monroe grabbed the pink slip stuck to the message needle at the front desk. The thing stood straight up – shiny and sharp – holding cancellations and rescheduled appointments.

"It's amazing someone doesn't get stabbed with this thing," she muttered as she read the slip. Leaning over the desk to check out her schedule she groaned. "Great! Now I have to skip my lunch hour to prepare for this rescheduled lesson! Darn it all." She scrunched her mouth into a snarl. It was 4:00 and usually her time to sit out on the plaza with her bag lunch watching the downtown business people scurry by to catch their bus or carpool. But a 5:00 appointment with no lesson plan would scratch those plans for now. Maybe she could catch a bite of her sandwich later between lessons. There was a ten minute break at the top of each hour. Not much time, but enough for a drink of water or a bathroom break if you were quick enough to get there before someone else did.

Kerri Blake stood at the corner of the desk and gave her a lopsided smirk. She was about a head taller than Sydney and with her three inch heels seemed to loom even taller. Her golden blond hair was pulled into a ponytail that draped fashionably on the side of her head. Her long slim skirt was in a navy blue shade with a slit up the back and topped with a softly draping winged sleeve white sweater. She gazed intently at the dance floor.

4:00 in the afternoon was usually a quiet time on the floor, and today was no exception. There was only one couple out in the middle of the floor with a soft disco melody playing in the background. Daniel Loggerman was chatting eagerly with a tall slender girl. Daniel was over six feet tall and this girl was almost as tall. Her wispy white blond hair was in stark contrast to his dark short neatly trimmed hair. They were laughing. Then he took her into dance position and began a slow romantic Rumba. She tittered nervously as he lifted his arm and lead her into an underarm turn. He guided her successfully under the arm and brought her back into a close dance position. She tittered again and began to turn her head looking behind her. Kerri stood closer to the dance floor and gave her a thumbs up and a nod.

"My sister," she explained. Sydney drew closer and watched for a moment.

"I guess you sort of look alike." She looked from one face to the other.

"Gwen. She's still in high school. We're about a year apart." Kerri explained briefly. "It's just Gwen, my dad and me. My mom died a few years ago, so Gwen and I are pretty close. I thought the dance lessons would be great for her. A way to feel more in touch with herself – a real confidence booster socially."

"She's very beautiful. Not really a high school looking girl at all," Sydney commented.

"I guess not," Kerri hesitated. "I guess not."

Sydney grabbed her dance programs and found a table out on the edge of the floor to plan her lessons. It was peaceful and the quiet lesson between Gwen and Daniel was nice for a distraction once in a while. It was a nice change from the usually loud, pounding music that was normally playing. Gwen seemed to be shy yet at the same time strong willed. In her own way, she was controlling the flow of the lesson without even saying anything at all. Her hair circled her head like a halo with the ends catching the sprinkling of light. She looked into Daniel's face and gave a smile – chin tilted slightly down and eyes fawnlike. Daniel may have noticed, but he continued to explain the step they were working on and withdrew emotionally from her glances.

Suzanna stood behind the reception desk and casually caught each teacher as they passed by. "Short meeting tonight after the last lesson. It won't last long."

The group of teachers crowded around the back teachers' office after the last student left. Joan had managed to shoo the last bunch of usually meandering students out the door on their way to a club for a nightcap. This particular group of young novice dancers had become socially close and tried to stand around casually after the last lesson to glean any gossip tidbits from staff conversations. Sometimes the staff felt their private lives were much the same as caged zoo animals – always on display. It didn't take long for new staff members to guard their outside lives very closely. One unguarded moment could cause undo trouble not only for that one person, but for the rest of the group as well. It had happened too many times.

Suzanna waited for them all to quiet down before making her announcements. "I know everything is in a bit of chaos with the death of Mr. Garrett, but we need to remember that the studio goes on as usual. Therefore, in a week and a half we have the regional convention in Chicago to attend." She waited for the groans to subside then continued. "We will all have to leave after the last lesson is over that Friday for the drive down to Chicago." Another set of groans. "I know it is a long and tedious ride, but we need to get ourselves back into the dance spirit and

59

let those of us who have won recognition from this organization be honored for their efforts." This brought a brief clap from those who might expect to receive some sort of award. "Now for the tricky part of this – Edward volunteered us to perform at this convention as he usually does." Groans again. "We need to prepare for this performance by using our daily dance sessions as well as afterhours rehearsals for this show. Go home tonight and enjoy one evening off but then get yourselves up for late night rehearsals. I will post the partner list by tomorrow morning. I have a fabulous idea for the routine." Suzanna with all her expertise in dance was normally not allowed to choreograph the staff routines for regional performances. Edward was very adamant about choreographing these routines as well as taking credit for their successes. "I have a piece of music that will be quite unique." The excitement in her voice was enough to catch everyone's attention and the room suddenly became quite still. "It's one song that uses ten different dances moving from Fox Trot to Waltz to Tango to Swing and so forth." There was a hush and then people began to slowly nod their heads as they thought through this idea. "It should be quite interesting. So let's get going on this routine. Megan?" She turned to Megan Meeker. Megan was one of the more colorful teachers.

She always looked impeccable with perfect make up, perfect hair, perfect dress and always a hat. She was known for her hats. In fact, her small efficiency apartment had one whole wall decorated with pegs holding hats. "Could you make a trip to one of the stores downtown here to look for appropriate dresses? We need something that is full and moves across the floor for the smooth dances as well as has some flash for the rhythm dances. We don't have much time, so we need enough of them for the entire staff of women. That might take some effort." Megan nodded.

"Thank you." Suzanna concluded the meeting.

"Daniel," Kerri grabbed his elbow before he had a chance to follow the group out the door and escape. "How do you think Gwen is doing with her dancing?" Kerri's eyes gleamed expectantly.

"She's doing just fine," Daniel nodded.

"She is becoming quite attached to you ...", her voice trailed off waiting for his comment.

"Luckily we have that rule 'Student Teacher fraternization prohibited'," he said referring to the sign in large bold letters that was tacked prominently to the reception desk. It was all too often that receptionist Morgan Canfield pointed to that sign as an infatuated student passed by or a new teacher gazed fondly at one of their better looking students. It was a clear reminder that socializing outside of the studio was in poor taste not only for the studio and its reputation, but for the teacher who might discover how devastating a relationship can be for a promising dance career.

Kerri sucked in her breath. Clearly she hadn't expected that response from Daniel. Daniel was charming and handsome. His students couldn't help becoming a bit too attached, and that had been a problem he had faced in the last studio where he worked.

Sydney and Antoine who were following Kerri and Daniel couldn't help but overhear the conversation and the expressions that were passing between the two. Daniel was cool and collected. Kerri was taken back by the response she had received from her attempt to retrieve Daniel's reaction to her sister, Gwen. He hadn't appeared flattered by Gwen's interest nor with any intention to pursue anything further.

Antoine caught Sydney's arm and pulled her back into the teachers' office. He held her for a moment or two and then whispered. "Daniel is gay. He hasn't told anyone here on the staff, but I saw him out at the club. He's rather quiet and probably wants to keep that part of his life away from the studio and the staff."

Any gossip was never safe with Antoine. He fairly burst with excitement whenever he had something he could pass on. This was his opportunity to do so. Sydney on the other hand was very closed mouthed about any personal news. Antoine's confession to her about Daniel's sexual preference would remain with her. She wouldn't reveal his secret to others on the staff. Especially Kerri. But it did make her more understanding about the struggle Sheila and Daniel were having as roommates. Everyone had assumed they were living together because of a personal relationship. That clearly was not the case at all. Sydney pondered that situation a bit more as she followed Antoine down the hall to escape for the evening.

X.

Sydney scanned the slip of paper taped to the wall of the teachers' office with the dance partner assignments and grinned. She was paired with Daniel. To be honest, there some partners who weren't exactly easy. One never made it to rehearsal and made the performance a real challenge. It always worked out somehow, but the worry prior to the event was harrowing. Another didn't shower and going through the rehearsals could be unbearable at times. Daniel was a gem. He was tall with perfect posture and always made his partner look good. He was always at rehearsals and even practiced during slow hours of the day. Yes, this was good.

Dressed in sweat pants and a t-shirt, Sydney waited out on the dance floor for the rest of the staff to arrive. Suzanna was perched behind the set of bongo drums by the sound system counting out the beats of her chosen song when Megan breezed in carrying hanging bags. Megan dressed in a flowing apricot skirt and matching silk blouse had been out shopping for costumes. Her short cut hair was covered with a felt apricot hat circled at the band with tiny flowers. She pulled off the plastic dress cover to reveal an emerald green dress.

"Sydney, go try this on for us," she motioned handing off the hanger. "Suzanna, I think this is going to be perfect..." she was saying.

The green dress had an ankle length full circle skirt, fitted waist and bodice with skinny straps that laced through the open back. Sydney swirled around the floor allowing the skirt fabric to float like a lily pad on a pond. Suzanna was nodding approval.

"It needs something more..." Suzanna pondered out loud.

"Just what I was thinking," Megan's full lips bowed up into a smile as she tugged a glittery belt from a small bag and fastened it around Sydney's waist. "There. Perfect."

"Did you hold enough for the group?" Suzanna asked. Megan nodded. "Men, you need to wear black tails."

"What about emerald green cummerbunds? I could whip some up by the end of the week?" Megan suggested.

"Sounds good." And that was that. The costumes had been selected, and Megan was clearly excited with her choices.

The rehearsal went well. Each dance took only a few seconds and a few quick amalgamations to master. It was a very clever concept that made learning the routine simpler than usual. Beginning with the entrance, the couples circled with a series of Fox Trot twinkles and syncopated turns. Then they moved into an elegant Waltz with advanced left turns and spirals. The dress sample looked great with the smooth dances moving in a circle around the room – the skirt twirling with each turn. The sultry Tango also moved around the room but provided the drama of romance with the ladies dancing a series of quick flares and a ronde around behind the man's back. After a few runs through this section, the rehearsal ended with plans to pick up the rhythm dances in the evening session.

Although additional practices could be tedious, working on new choreography made the day more enjoyable. Sydney and Daniel took a few moments between lessons to quickly rehearse the portions they had learned that morning. Each time through gave them more confidence and a giddiness that lasted until the ten o'clock practice. This time however, the practice would become more complicated. The amalgamations were again easy to learn – quick snippets of each dance. The difficulty would be in moving each couple to their places on the floor. While the smooth dances moved in a circle like cars driving around the turnpike, the rhythm dances allowed each couple to dance in a small territorial spot on the floor. The trick was getting to that spot. The Tango would be arranged so the flares and rondes faced in different directions allowing each couple a few needed steps to move into position. They tried several solutions to this problem and finally reached one that was suitable.

At the end of the rehearsal, Sydney grabbed her bag and followed Suzanna and Antoine out the door toward the bus stop. It was dark and beginning cool down, so she wanted to stick closely with the group. Suzanna and Antoine would get off a few stops before Sydney and Carson. It had become a nightly ritual.

"I heard from the police today," Suzanna was saying to Antoine as they waited at the bus stop. He leaned in a little closer to hear the details.

"Edward was murdered."

"As we suspected," he shrugged.

"Yes, but the way he was murdered is the surprise." She waited a moment for him to turn toward her. Sydney and Carson crowded in.

"He was struck on the head. From behind. Then he was run over with a car. They are at this point unsure whether the car was driven by the killer or just some random driver coming down the street."

"Wouldn't a random driver notice they had struck something?" Carson asked. "Especially something as large as a person?"

Everyone nodded in unison. "And why was Edward going out the front door?" Sydney piped up. "He never goes out the front that I've ever seen. Always the back door."

"Could be he was going out – you know, to a late night dinner or to a club. Sometimes he does that." Antoine added. There was mumbling agreement then the bus pulled up and the conversation dropped.

By the end of the week the choreography was complete, and the rehearsals more intense going into the final phases of dancing in unison. The dresses were fitted and tuxes ready. Everything was set for the long drive to Chicago. "Let's try a last run through people," Suzanna clapped her hands trying to get everyone onto the dance floor before they left. Wiggling and giggling, they got into places and the music started. Suddenly just as they started into the Viennese Waltz something happened.

"Hey, we're off time," Antoine scowled. "What happened?"

They began again, and again the same thing happened. "It's a damn skip in the record," Suzanna moaned. "Now what? We only have one recording of this and this is it. It's not a record we could find in a store. I had to order it specially."

"Hey look at this," Antoine took his partner Megan and started the Viennese waltz section, held a curtsy and continued on. "See we change the choreography to fit the skip. Here, try this everyone." They all gathered close behind the two and began to practice the new sequence. "It'll work," Suzanna sighed a relief. "It'll work. Everyone got it. Please don't forget."

They all gathered up their bags and met in the back of the parking ramp. The group would drive in two or three cars after the final lesson was completed on Friday night. They would drive all night until they reached Chicago in the morning. Not everyone had a driver's license. With the bus such a viable and cheap means of transportation, some had never bothered to take a driver's test. Meagan and Suzanna didn't drive at all. Sydney preferred not to drive, and Sheila hadn't changed her out of state license over to a Minnesota license yet. So each car was arranged with two to three drivers who would switch off during the night. In years past, they had used Edward's big Cadillac because it held so many passengers, but that wouldn't work this time. They opted to caravan together using three smaller cars owned by Antoine, Joan, and Carson. One year one of the cars had been picked up for speeding and had spent a good deal of time sitting in the local police station trying to scrape together enough money to pay the fine before they were allowed to finish the journey. This year they didn't want a repeat of that incident.

The Chicago hotel was large with old fashioned elegance as the cars pulled up to a glorious sunrise in the distant sky. Already several studios from all parts of the Midwest had arrived for the Convention. As they entered carrying garment and smaller duffle bags, the teachers who had been with the studio for a while greeted and hugged some of the dancers they had met previously at past conventions. The long car ride was forgotten when they met old friends and began to catch up on the last year. Of course many had heard about Edward Garrett's death. There were questions and not much to report to the curious. Could it be one of them? The thought suddenly began to materialize in some of their minds as the questions came – had they ridden to Chicago in the same car with a murderer? Which one of this group wasn't completely trustworthy? And who knew something they weren't telling?

There would be three to a room with only a few minutes to unpack before dance session was scheduled to begin. The instructor this weekend was Damian Vito. Damian was becoming known as the best Latin dancer and instructor in the country. He was frequently called on for coaching and judging in Europe – something that was not the norm for American dancers. The International dance standard was not as well known in America. The United States had an American style that was only commonly danced in this country and was now starting to infiltrate into the dance styles of other countries known for their International style of dance. The two styles were now becoming more common among dancers worldwide and no longer a difference that split the continents into what was considered "proper" for ballroom dancing.

The hotel ballroom on the main floor of the hotel was quickly filling up with couples ready to dance. Some were nursing cups of coffee. Others were limbering up with stretches along the walls. Still others were chatting and catching up on news. The air was electric. Damian Vito started the session by having the whole group surround him. He demonstrated some of the new amalgamations he was putting together for the new dance syllabus that would be coming out by the end of the year.

The beginning patterns were quite easy for most although there were some teachers who were very inexperienced. Any pattern would be a challenge for them. They quickly moved on to the more advanced steps. People would ooh and aah when Damian would demonstrate a new figure.

"Let's separate into three groups so everyone has a chance to use more of the dance floor. These couples over here stay standing on the floor. Those to my left sit down and wait for the second wave of dancing. And to my right sit down. You will be last." Damian waved his arms and waited for the groups to get into their places before he turned on the music. He was a short dark haired man in his late thirties who neither looked like a dancer in stature nor in his temperament. He was round and not the muscular athletic looking person you would expect to be a famous dancer. But when he pulled another teacher from his studio into dance position to demonstrate the final combination they had learned, he was electric. His movement was perfectly controlled. His body shaped into the most esthetic alignments, and his partner lead into every step with ease. It was magical and most difficult for the first group of dancers to stop staring at the demonstrating couple to get up and do the step themselves.

Sydney, Antoine, and Megan were seated on the floor – placed in the third group. Megan and Antoine had paired together, and Sydney was dancing with another teacher form a smaller Wisconsin town. Megan gasped as the first group began dancing.

"Look over there," she motioned without trying to point.

"Where?" Sydney tried to follow her gaze but didn't see much other than people on the floor dancing.

"That woman has no underwear on. And when her partner twirls her you can see everything underneath her skirt," she hissed.

Sure enough, an older stocky gentleman was twirling a young woman who looked to be in her late teens or early twenties. As she spun around, her skirt lifted showing those seated on the floor a full view of her sheer pantyhose with no underwear.

"Oh, my god," Antoine was shuddering as she began dancing in front of them. "That is the most disgusting thing I have ever seen." He turned his head and wouldn't look back toward the dance floor.

XI.

Before dinner, Sydney and Megan were hanging their dresses and accessories for the evening's routine. They would all take their garment bags and dance shoes down to the ballroom during dinner so they would be able to quickly change before the performance. Antoine was sitting in front of the mirror chatting away about the disgusting scene they had witnessed that day during the dance session.

"He had to be a dance owner," he was saying. "She was probably his only teacher. She's young and probably impressed by his knowledge of dance - so easily seduced by him. Disgusting to use your power like that."

"Do you think Edward was like that?" Sydney asked. "You know. Using his power to seduce young girls."

"Oh yes. Of course he was. He just was more suave about it. That old guy had a pot belly and was bald and just plain disgusting." Antoine made a face.

"Well, Edward was old and bald..." Megan began to say.

"Yes, but no one knew it. At least not unless you were around the studio for a while. He hid it pretty well.

He dressed well… he was charming." Antoine swished his hands at "charming".

"I guess. At least he tried to be in the beginning." Sydney sneered. She didn't want to tell anyone about the Tango incident. It was humiliating and ugly. Yet how many more had experienced something similar? "Do you think he was killed because he was like that old guy. Because he seduced the wrong girl?"

"Could be. Who knows. Who has a car? Maybe we should look for the car. I think someone who wasn't involved in the murder would certainly report hitting someone, so it has to be someone who actually was involved in the murder. That's my opinion." Megan smoothed out her skirt and hung her glittery belt around the hanger.

"Well, that leaves you out," Antoine laughed.

"Yes, it does. And Suzanna," she added.

"And Sheila," Sydney piped up.

The room was silent. "Maybe," Antoine muttered.

The ballroom was transformed. There were dozens of round tables covered in snow white table clothes with place settings of china and neatly folded linen napkins. In the center of each table was a beautiful centerpiece of colorful flowers. At the far end of the ballroom was a long table for the studio owners and distinguished guests. Each studio had a table with place cards at each seat. Teachers dressed in elegant evening wear and tuxes or suits milled around the floor carefully checking each table for their name.

"Oh, my," Sheila sighed as she entered. "This is just glorious. So elegant." Her hand pressed her heart. She tossed her red mane of hair to the side and adjusted the pearl necklace she had chosen to wear with her pink lace evening dress. It was a hot pink short dress with a pink lace cover up. She smiled coyly at a studio owner who was passing to get to the table of honor at the front. "Where is my seat?" she asked fluttering her eyelashes.

"You're over here by me," Megan announced. Their seats were on the side facing the owners' table right by the door to the hallway. "Let me share something special with you." She leaned in close to Sheila and whispered loudly so the rest of the table was able to hear what she was saying.

"There is a tradition that occurs every year at this Convention. And because you are our Supervisor, we want to let you be included in the tradition."

"Oh, yes," Sheila again clutched at her heart. "What is it?"

"When the owner of the Chicago studio gets up to greet all of the studios, we have a way of letting everyone know who each teacher is. It's like a cheer that announces our names. Because Minneapolis studio is the largest, we always start the cheer and then it passes on from table to table until everyone is introduced. For example, I would stand up and shout 'I'm Megan from Minneapolis.' Then I would sit down and the person next to me stands and announces their name. Everyone cheers and claps. It's all great fun." Megan demonstrated a cheering motion.

"Sounds like fun." Sheila looked around and her eyes came to Suzanna who was seated at the owners' table to the right of the Chicago owner, a large burly man dressed in a tuxedo and a black shiny cummerbund. He had a dark thin mustache and was smiling at Suzanna as she sipped her water. His glossy black hair was slicked back from his forehead.

Megan noticed Sheila's momentary frown and added, "Because you are the Supervisor of the Minneapolis studio, I think you should begin the introductions."

"I'd love to," Sheila said teeth gritted without looking away from Suzanna. "It would be my pleasure."

The teachers at the table remained hushed and waited as everyone took their seats. The owner at the front podium blew loudly into the microphone causing a slight high pitched screech. "As the owner of the Chicago studio I would like to greet all of our guests."

Before the group could start a weak clap, Sheila jumped to her feet and shouted, "Minneapolis studio thanks you! I'm Sheila Pickford!" She waved her arms wildly – more animated than Megan had demonstrated. The eyes of the crowd all turned to stare at the red head in the hot pink dress. The remainder of the teachers sitting at the table sat stone faced and not moving. Sheila turned to Megan seated at her right and waited for her to follow which of course she didn't. Horrified that she had made such a spectacle of herself and finally realizing that she had been duped by her staff, she turned to run out of the room. But of course when things start badly, they continue badly. She caught her shoe on her chair and fell sprawling across the floor. Sobbing at the added indignation, she managed to rise and sprint out the door to safety.

The whole room began to murmur, and the Minneapolis tables burst into laughter – although it was quiet so as not to bring any more attention than there already was to this end of the room. Suzanna sat and stared, her head cocked to one side and her lips pursed.

As the room noise began to die down and the waiters served the salads to the tables, Morgan rose from the next table and left following Sheila. She found her in the ladies' room sobbing and dabbing black mascara from under her eyes.

"So I suppose you came in to gloat and laugh," Sheila drawled as she stared into the mirror and noticed Morgan standing behind her.

"No, not really," Morgan wore a beige skirt and jacket with a striped T-shirt. Her hair was neatly parted but she wore no makeup except for a natural toned lip stick that Suzanna had probably made her wear. "You know when you started at the studio, I really didn't like you very much. You were arrogant and pushy. I'm sure that's how the rest of the staff saw you as well. Especially Suzanna. But she never said anything even though you took her job with no qualms and a good chunk of her income as well." Morgan sucked in her breath and waited for Sheila to react, but the puffy red faced woman didn't say a word.

"But as time went on, I began to soften. I even began to like you – at least I tried to understand you. And I'm here to say sorry for what happened in there. Did you deserve it? Maybe. You haven't treated anyone in the studio with much respect, but as I said, I'm here to say sorry. I hope this ends here and now. I hope you begin to be a respected leader like I think you'd like to be. But it's going to take some changes from you to get there. I think you need to recognize that Suzanna is one classy lady – someone who has enough guts to let you hang yourself without doing anything revengeful for what you did to her. And you'll hang yourself just from the way you treat others if you don't straighten up and change. That means wiping off your eyes, taking a deep breath and going right back in there. Laugh at yourself and show them they can't break you. Then laugh with them again and let it go." There was silence. "Let me give you a hug, and we can go back together."

Sheila hesitated. Then she let Morgan give her a hug. She straightened up, wiped her eyes, and said "Thanks." It was no more than a whisper, but it was enough. They walked back in just in time for the chicken surprise to be served. Megan looked intently at her plate, but didn't say anything. Her bright red full lips curled up in a quiet smile. Within a few moments, conversation was flowing and all was forgotten. Morgan watched from her table and made eye contact occasionally with Sheila giving

80

her a nod and a smile. "Keep going," she was saying. "Just keep it going."

When dinner was done and the plates cleared from the tables, the presentation of awards began. Suzanna accepted an award for the highest grossing studio. Antoine was awarded a second place Counselor award, and Megan was honored as first place Specialist. There was a moment of silence for Edward Garrett at the end of the ceremony and then a break before the performances. A rumble of chairs left teachers racing for the rest rooms and the Minneapolis staff gathering up their garment bags in the back of the room to change clothes.

A tall thin studio owner from a small Midwest town stopped momentarily to speak to Kerri. She reached down to pick up her garment bag clearly marked in large white letters with BLAKE. "Hello." He grinned looking intently at her first and then her bag. She tossed her blond hair to the side and waited for him to speak. "Are you the BLAKE from the Blake Hotel?" He tried to charm a smile as he gazed into her blue eyes.

"I suppose so. My father owns the Blake Hotel. Why do you ask?" Her stare turned into a glare.

"Oh no reason. Just thought I'd ask." And he turned abruptly and walked off with a devilish grin on his face.

"Your father owns the Blake?" Sydney asked trying to make sense of the whole scene.

Kerri just nodded and grabbed her bag angrily. "Who was that man?"

Before anyone could answer, Suzanna broke away from the owners who were congratulating her on her studio award to gather her group of teachers. "I don't know what all of that table stuff was, and I don't want to know. I do know that I want all of you to get yourselves together – as a group. Because when we – or you – do this routine, it's important that it all comes together. It's important for my career of course to début a great routine, but it is equally as important for you to perform a great routine. It could mean a successful dance career for you. Needless to say, if you decide your differences are more important than this performance, it could also mean the end of your careers. So just think it over before you get out on that floor." Suzanna pursed her mouth and stared over her round glasses. Her black evening dress had an uneven hem cut that swept from a long edge on the right to a shorter hem on the left. She chose to cover her thin arms with long sleeves

82

that were lacy and smartly tipped over the back of her tiny hands.

"It's over. It's done and you need not worry about this performance," Sheila said steadily with no hint of a drawl. Megan looked at the floor and nodded slowly. "Done," she repeated.

The group snatched up their costumes and trotted off to find more accessible places to change in the restrooms on other floors of the hotel. Suzanna turned with a smile to greet the man who was tapping her shoulder. "Oh, Charles. How are you?" Her hand pressed to cover her mouth only for a second before she let the fake smile again appear across her face and the conversation continued.

It was just over an hour before the ballroom was once again filled with people. Some had changed into more casual clothes. Others still wore the cocktail dresses and tuxes they had worn for dinner having spent the last hour in the bar talking with old friends and sipping cold drinks. Tonight would be their night. Music playing and for a change the teachers actually dancing, not with their students, but with each other. It was a time they waited for all year. Dancing was no longer work but play. The Chicago studio owner once again rumbled forward taking his place at the microphone. This time when he greeted the guests, they all cheered. The formal air had subsided and the social hour was beginning. He announced the Minneapolis studio performance and let people take their seats. The lights dimmed and the dancers snaked out to the front to begin their entrance to the floor. The music began and the routine started - slow and elegant moving through each dance bringing applause and shouts as they broke into a each new dance rhythm. They artfully moved through the skip in the record and when they reached the end pose, each couple doing a different lift, the crowd rewarded them with wild claps and whistling. Sydney was perched up on Daniel's shoulder – the top of the formation and Sheila was dipped to the floor in a long elegant pose – one leg draped seductively over the other.

Suzanna sighed a relief and looked considerably more at ease. Studio owners began moving toward her to give her their congratulations and asking where she had found such a "fabulous" piece of music. She smiled.

Morgan watched Sheila stand back by the door staring at Suzanna for a moment. Her eyes narrowed and her lips pressed together. It was at that instant that Morgan realized how much Sheila envied and hated the woman she had pushed out. But why? She hadn't known Suzanna before moving to Minneapolis, had she?

Sheila felt someone grab her elbow and pull her gently toward the hallway. "Let's get a drink," Morgan said maneuvering Sheila through the crowd gathered at the door. They found their way out and headed toward the small hotel bar located toward the entryway. After they took seats at the bar and ordered drinks, Morgan began.

"I guess you didn't take what I said earlier very seriously," she said stirring the glass of golden liquid and ice on the tiny hotel napkin.

"I don't think I quite know what you are referring to," Sheila drawled lifting her margarita glass with the salted edge to her lips.

"You think Suzanna planned that joke to humiliate you, don't you!" Morgan stated flatly.

"Well, I suppose I do."

"Sorry to burst your revengeful bubble, but Suzanna is too much of a professional and a classy lady to allow something like that to happen – even to you. No, I think the teachers cooked that little plan up all on their own. And I want to take back my earlier apology. You did deserve that. After all you've done to this staff and this studio…".

"Now wait a cotton pickin' minute. What **I've** done to this staff and studio? What are you talking about?" Sheila put her glass down and jutted her chin out.

"Each and every teacher on our staff has more experience than you do. It's easy to see. You are a novice – a beginner. And they all know that. You've proven over and over that you have no idea what you are doing as a dancer or as a supervisor. You are taking money out of their pockets by being incompetent. You don't know how to coach their lessons nor do you know how to sell dance lessons. They know that, and it's about time you know that too. They have to wonder why Edward Garrett would put you in this position. What did you to do to get him to offer you such a plum job that you have no business having? Tell me. What was it?" Morgan didn't mince words. She laid it on the line and waited for an answer.

"I don't have to take this! It's an outrage…" Sheila sputtered.

"No you don't. But if you don't face it pretty soon, you'll end up like Edward. No longer around."

"Are you threatening me lady?" Sheila leaned over and glared.

"Not at all. I'm just telling you the truth. Now be a big enough person to listen to the truth and figure out how you can do some good rather than continually irritating everyone around you. All I hear is complaining from you. That and stupid mistakes like the one today. You listened to someone because they stroked your ego. What's the matter with you? Can't you see anything that goes on around you? Are you blind as well." Morgan wanted to go on, but decided to let the words sink in first. Too much would do no good.

Sheila's whole body crumbled. She leaned on the bar burying her head in her arms for a moment. Then she looked up. "I didn't do anything to or for Edward Garrett to get this job. Maybe I implied that something would happen, but it never really did. I guess after I got to Minneapolis, he had other things he was concerned about and forgot about me all together. He never checked to see if I was all that I said I was. He didn't even check on the financial condition of my department. I assumed that Suzanna would inform him, but I guess she didn't. She didn't do anything to help me..." Sheila's voice turned angry.

"And what was she suppose to do to help you? Do your job for you? You took her job – her income – her title – her career. What should she do for you? You are the villain in this story. Not the victim. Do you see yourself as the poor misunderstood **victim**? How does that work?" Morgan was repulsed by Sheila's response.

"So what am I suppose to do?"

"Maybe you should be the one to apologize. Suzanna saved your butt back there. She stood up for you when the rest of the staff could be having you for lunch and spitting you out. This could have been just the beginning of your humiliation. But now because of Suzanna, it's the end. How lucky are you?" Morgan slammed her glass down on the napkin. "I have to wonder how many of those teachers think you might have something to do with Edward's death. Have you bothered to think about that? Or maybe you really did kill him. You have enough anger as far as I can see."

Sheila turned pale. "I swear, I had nothing to do with Edward's murder. I don't want anyone to connect me with such a thing." Instead of the anger she displayed during the beginning of the conversation, Sheila now softened. Her eyes began to close and she sat still thinking about all that had been said. "Yes, you are right. I need to deal with this whole thing right now. It's getting out of hand. I agree. I need to apologize."

Reality can be sobering thought Morgan. She reached over and patted her hand.

Kerri Blake walked into the bar and looked around. She may have seen Morgan and Sheila at the bar but chose not to acknowledge their presence. She walked toward the back of the bar and stood in the shadow of the entrance to the small rest room. A moment later, a man entered and looked around. His grin turned to confusion as his head flicked left then right. He was about five nine, a good couple of inches shorter than Kerri Blake. He was slender and about forty with blond turning gray hair combed back away from his face in waves. His face would have been considered a baby face except for the creases on his forehead and around his eyes. He wore a white starched dress shirt unbuttoned at the collar and neatly pressed black pants. His black dance shoes had a Cuban heel to make him appear taller than he was. As he turned away from the doorway and began to scan the dark bar, a voice hissed in his ear.

"Why are you following me?" Kerry Blake was standing behind his shoulder and created a nervous jerk from the man. But he didn't look behind him. Instead, a slow grin spread across his face and he simply waited. After a moment, he turned but there was no one behind him. He looked confused and left the bar.

Morgan returned to the ballroom leaving Sheila to do a little soul searching. The Minneapolis staff was out on the floor dancing and laughing with the glittery disco ball twirling above creating small sparkles of light flickering across the floor. Morgan squinted through the darkness and located Suzanna across the floor sitting at a back table with Carson and Sydney. She began to weave through the crowd to that corner. Touching Suzanna's shoulder she pointed out across the floor.

"Do you know who that man is?" She fingered the man who had been following Kerri Blake. He was standing on the other side of the room again looking slowly around stopping occasionally to squint before continuing with his search.

"That's Dennis Whit. He used to be a teacher at our studio when I first started. He now owns a studio in Iowa. Why?" Suzanna spoke cupping her hand so Morgan could hear over the beat of the music.

"I think he's following Kerri. I saw him twice approach her."

"That's odd," Suzanna frowned. She waited a moment to think that through then pulled Morgan's arm closer. "I used to date Dennis Whitmore, that's his real name before Edward made him change it. Shortened it so it wouldn't be so complicated. That was pretty common back then. It's not done much anymore."

Hmmm. Morgan looked over at Carson and Sydney. They were trying to eavesdrop on the conversation, but only caught snippets.

"Sydney, do you think you could do a little spying for me? I'm just curious as to why Mr. Whit made Kerri so angry. He saw me both times during their conversations, so I don't think I can approach him. But you could. He might talk to you about what he's doing and why he is so interested in Kerri." Morgan flipped her head in the direction of Dennis Whit.

"Sure. I've met Dennis before. I could talk with him." She nodded and stood up to wander across the room. She said something to him and the two went out to the dance floor for a Samba. Morgan sat down between Carson and Suzanna.

"So you dated Dennis?" Morgan asked.

"We actually lived together. It started out as a friendship – a way to save money. But it grew into more than that. We were quite a couple on the dance floor. We were Edward's stars." Suzanna smiled. "It was a good time and a stressful time as well. Edward made it difficult for us most of the time – always creating tension and a competition between us to see who could do better. I was the Supervisor and Dennis was the Counselor. So we were always trying to outdo each other in the business and trying to get more recognition on the dance floor too. Edward saw to it that we were always at each other's throats when we were in the studio. Eventually it came home with us. When Edward offered Dennis the opportunity to buy a studio with him, it ended our relationship. If it hadn't been for Edward, we might still be together. And happy, I might add." Suzanna's eyes were sad.

Morgan could imagine the two. Both small and thin. A perfect physical match as dance partners. She hadn't thought of Suzanna as a perfect match for any man. But Dennis was just the person who would fit Suzanna. There was a heavy air of sadness after that conversation ended. The three of them watched Sydney dancing with Dennis in the middle of the floor. He was good. His body seemed to move in ways that most didn't. He had a flexibility and a rhythm that was addicting to watch. Sydney was laughing and having a great time with him. Kerri Blake was nowhere in sight.

After the music ended, Dennis steered Sydney back toward the table and her seat. Then with a quick gesture of his hands he signed something to Suzanna. She signed back and got up to meet him in the middle of the floor. They began a quick Cha Cha that nearly cleared the dance floor. People crowded to each side to watch them perform. Suzanna was laughing at the familiar dance moves she had not danced for such a long time. When the music ended, Dennis gathered her into his arms for a slow and romantic Rumba.

Sydney took her seat with Carson sandwiched between her and Morgan. He pulled back slightly to let them talk. Carson Hunter was in his early thirties with a long dark ponytail and a short frame that didn't show off any muscle. Sydney and Carson had attended the same college but hadn't become friends until meeting at the dance studio. Edward was always chiding Carson for his laid back nature and lack of fashion sense. He referred to him as "the hippie" and always flashed him an annoying peace sign whenever he passed him just to see if he could get a reaction. It didn't. But Carson's brilliant mind had quickly made him a master of dance patterns and technique. He was the one who could answer any challenging question about the degree of turn or which part of the foot was used when doing a back spot turn. Quiet and amiable, Carson was clearly everyone's good friend.

"Dennis said he got a call from Edward a few days before his death," Sydney began. "They were talking about financial matters and Edward mentioned he had a connection to some big money that would pull the studio out of its financial troubles. He was getting close to the daughter of the Blake Hotel owner. When he saw Kerri's bag with "BLAKE" written on it, he began to connect the conversation with her."

"That would make sense," Carson muttered. "Dennis and Edward became partners when Dennis had ideas about quitting and starting his own studio. I was just starting at the studio when the whole thing was just about to blow. Edward convinced Dennis to go into a partnership with him in a closed down studio in some small Iowa town. Dennis didn't have much start up money, so the offer seemed pretty good at the time. When he got down to Iowa, Edward's promise of financial support didn't come through. Edward was always in a financial hardship – not because the studio wasn't doing well, but because he had expensive tastes. He was always taking exotic vacations and heading off to Italy to buy clothes and shoes. He had an extensive and pricey art collection. Edward basically spent all of the money the studio ever made and then blamed hardship on the staff and their lack of ambition.

Suzanna knew the truth, and Dennis soon discovered a new version of the truth. He worked his butt off and made a go of the studio in Iowa finally buying out Edward. Edward didn't want to sell, but was always in moments of desperation. It would seem logical that they would discuss financial matters."

Morgan pondered. "I guess if we want to find out who murdered Edward Garrett, we might have to follow the money, as they say." Both Sydney and Carson nodded.

Dennis and Suzanna spent the remainder of the evening dancing and laughing and reconnecting. Sydney began to feel tired from the long trip and went to bed. Carson, a night owl anyway would stay up with Morgan until the music stopped playing. Antoine and Daniel didn't make an appearance again after the earlier performance was finished. Megan sat at a table with one of the other studios for a while and then meandered off to bed. Sheila and Kerri disappeared as well. They were rooming with Joan. All three seemed to vanish only to reappear the next morning for the dance session that Damian Vito was conducting on the Bolero.

Damian demonstrated a new and interesting technique for the slow romantic dance from Cuba. Instead of the stiff upright style that prevailed for so many years, he put a flow and lift to the dance creating the sensuality that was missing. He oozed with body movement and a closed – opened position with his partner. The traditional hockey stick motion was now flowing with rise and fall. Everyone was eager to try the new style.

Suzanna came down to the ballroom with Dennis. The two of them immediately got into a dance position and began to implement the new Bolero movements. They looked happy. They also looked to be very good dancers.

Sydney and Carson tried the new style – struggling quite a bit more than Dennis and Suzanna with the up and down motion. Morgan and Joan sat out the session, watching from a corner table with cups of steaming coffee and plates of big fat glazed donuts in front of them. Sheila was huddled in a fluffy cashmere sweater with her arms wrapped around her. Her hair was not as perfect as usual. A few red strands were draping across her face. Her usually perfect makeup was nonexistent. But she didn't look angry. Instead she had a calmness that she hadn't shown before.

Antoine wandered in and joined Morgan and Joan at their table. Daniel was nowhere to be seen. Megan and Kerri were dancing with each other. Megan was trying to lead Kerri without much success. After a frustrating try at the hockey stick maneuver, Megan motioned to Dennis for help. Kerri stiffened, but let Dennis lead her in the step. They looked rather odd out on the floor – Kerri about a head taller than Dennis. Kerri, with a perfect long legged model body, made Dennis appear small and way too slender. No matter, he lead her through the movement with ease.

Suzanna introduced the two of them. "Kerri Blake, this is Dennis Whit. He used to manage the Minneapolis studio and now owns a studio in Iowa. We were …partners for a while." She hesitated at this last statement. Dennis didn't look at Suzanna. He seemed used to this explanation of their relationship.

Kerri starred at the two of them and then smiled briefly. Who knows what she was thinking. Did she seem relieved that this wasn't a stalker or did she know everything already? Had someone spoken with her after her evening encounter to tell her who this man was? She didn't seem surprised, but she was by no means relaxed.

The session lasted a few more hours and after lunch, the group grabbed their belongings and headed for the cars to drive home. Suzanna and Dennis said a good-by, and she squeezed into Antoine's car. Antoine seemed excited. "Well? Are you two an item again?"

"He has a girlfriend. In Iowa. Tall, leggy and blond." Then she snuggled down to sleep.

PART II.

I.

Antoine climbed wearily up the stairs to his apartment after dropping off his riders. His bags felt heavy and the effects of driving and last night had begun to catch up to him. He put down his bags to fish out his door keys from his pocket when he was startled by a "Boo" behind him.

Amanda Garrett stood in her doorway – hair piled on top of her head in a curly mass, no makeup, and sweats with gaping holes. "Hi there," she grinned leaning against the door frame. "How was the trip?"

"Tiring," Antoine sighed. "Care for a drink? I could use one after the drive."

Amanda grabbed the Sunday paper rolled up on his doorstep and followed him into the dark apartment. He dropped his bags on an overstuffed chair in the corner and headed for the kitchen. Amanda curled up on the couch and unfolded the paper on the coffee table in front of her. Antoine carried two glasses of white wine and scooted in beside her.

"Take a look at today's spread." Amanda carefully open the front section of the paper to the inside

99

advertisement. There in black and white with arms joined and pouting expressions were Amanda and Kerri. Both tall and slender, they were wearing tall heeled boots, gauzy patterned skirts that swirled in the wind and halter tops. The fans used in the photo shoot blew Kerri's hair out behind her. Amanda's curls moved back away from her classic face.

"Love the boots. Hate the top," Antoine nodded. "Speaking of Kerri. Guess who was in Chicago?"

Amanda shook her head and held her gaze to the photo analyzing the pose. "Dennis." Antoine noticed Amanda's disinterest. Dennis and Amanda were never good friends. "The interesting part about this story is what Dennis said about Edward." That piqued her interest.

"What did Dennis say about Edward?" Amanda's expression became strangely curious. Antoine picked up his wine glass and took a sip. "What did Dennis say?" she repeated becoming a bit testy at having her query ignored.

"He said that Edward called him a few days before his death." Again Antoine lifted his glass to his lips and waited.

"So?" Amanda was now staring at Antoine and leaning in to listen.

"Dennis said Edward was getting close to the Blake Hotel money." Antoine again sipped his wine and waited.

"The Blake Hotel money? Meaning Kerri Blake? I don't think so. I would certainly know if Edward was seeing Kerri. I **know** those things." Amanda stood and began to pace the floor. "Ridiculous! Absolutely not! She's way too young for him."

"Amanda dear, you didn't even know when Edward was seeing Elenor and she was even younger," Antoine mentioned quietly the woman who had ended Amanda's and Edward's marriage. He had gotten a reaction and right now he was wondering why he had said this to his friend. Did he want to see what she would say? "Why are you concerned about Edward and anyone else anyhow? You've been over him for a long time."

"I am over him. It's just disturbing to think about him with Elenor or Kerri or anyone else that I have in my own circle of friends. If it was someone I didn't know it would be different. It's too close. Too close, that's all. And they are such babies." Amanda stopped her pacing and plopped down on the sofa again shaking her head.

"You aren't concerned about age, are you?" Antoine hesitated before asking.

"I'm a model. Of course I'm concerned about age. I'm thirty. That's over the hill for a model. It's lucky that I'm in that ad at all. There's a nineteen year old child standing next to me." She pointed a slender finger at the photo on the table. "Yes, I'm lucky to be there. And I'm lucky to be in next week's ad and the week after that. When my time runs out, what will I do then? Edward's no longer my husband so I have no financial interest vested in the studio or the dance business. What will I do?"

"Amanda, Edward is dead. He doesn't have the studio or a dance business anymore either."

Amanda heaved a deep sigh and buried her head in her arms. She didn't sob, but stayed in a cocoon position for a few moments. Antoine sat staring wondering what he should say. So he just said nothing. This was awkward. He had definitely said some things he shouldn't have said.

"I'm OK," Amanda came up for a breath of air. "Let's just forget we had this conversation. Let's just forget about Kerri Blake, the studio and my worry about growing old. I'm a resourceful person. I have a future...some place." She smiled a clamped lipped smile and took her wine glass. "I'll just take this on home for a night cap. You need some sleep after your trip." And she was gone. The paper remained on the table opened to the advertisement.

II.

Morgan Canfield was the first one in on Monday morning. The usual group of exercise models hadn't shown up this morning. The studio was eerily quiet. Flipping on all the lights and carrying a cup of coffee from the coffee shop down the street, she sat at the front desk to gaze over the appointments for the week. The weekend in Chicago hadn't been much of a physically exhausting trip for her – she hadn't danced and partied too late after receiving an award as the others had. She was just the receptionist. It hadn't been a strain for her. Today would be a quiet day she surmised. Everyone would come dragging in late and try desperately to just get through their teaching day. She was surprised to spot Sheila Pickford strolling through the front door earlier than usual.

Sheila had replaced her thin coat with a warm coat sweater with a full collar wrapped around her slender neck. She smiled. "Good morning!" She was way too friendly. What was going on?

"I just want to thank you," she began as she leaned over the front desk to view her schedule. "You stuck up for me and said some difficult things this weekend. I guess I needed all of that. I don't know why, but I feel good. I feel better about the studio, about the people who work here and about Daniel."

"And why is that?" Morgan inquired curiously.

"Because I am thinking about moving out of my apartment and leaving Daniel to fend for himself. He can deal with the rent. He can bring his sleazy friends over and let them stay as long as they like. I am moving out!" She lifted her head defiantly and with an air of satisfaction.

"And where will you go?"

"I don't know. But I will find some place," she said with a pound of her fist on the top of the desk.

"I may regret saying this but you could move in with me. It's so close that moving your things would be easy. Besides, it would save me lots of money to have a roommate." Morgan almost tried to hold her breath. Why had she said that? It had just come out without any effort. What was going on?

"Thanks. That would be very nice, and I think I'll take you up on that offer. I'll let Daniel know today and move in this evening after work. I don't have much to move. I haven't been here long enough to accumulate much stuff." Her drawl was grateful and calm. "I'll call Joan's mother this morning to let her know about the change." Then she walked back to the office with a strange lightness in her gait.

Morgan watched her move down the hall and began shaking her head. "I may regret this…".

"Regret what?" Sydney had stepped inside the door at just that moment. Her cheeks were pink from the cool morning. She began to unbutton her coat and shake the chill from her collar. "What will you regret?"

"I just asked Sheila to move in with me. Am I crazy? Will I regret it?" Morgan shook her head in disbelief.

"Probably." Then Sydney hung her coat on the coat rack, gave her a quick smile and pranced off to prepare for her lessons.

"Probably," Morgan repeated.

The remainder of the staff dragged in over the next half hour and said very little except to smile occasionally about something funny that had happened over the weekend. Most had some experience to share or some observations to make. It was a quiet day.

Sydney stared at Antoine not wanting to begin the task of planning her lessons. Her mind was going to the murder of Edward Garrett. Things that had happened this weekend flashed in her mind. They both sat at the round tables in the ballroom with paperwork and programs scattered in front of them. "Antoine, what about the car thing?" she wondered.

"What are you talking about?" he squinted across the table as the afternoon sun made a glare on the glass table top.

"Remember Edward was struck by a car after he was hit in the head? Who ran over him? There must be some type of evidence of damage to the car if it struck a person?" she pondered out loud.

"Most likely," he agreed.

She got up from the table, unfastened the straps to her ballroom shoes and slipped them off. She lightly scampered down the hall to the office and came back with the athletic shoes she wore in to work each day along with her coat.

"And where do you think you are going?" he demanded.

"Out to the parking lot to take a look at the cars. I want to check the front of the cars to see if I can spot any damage. It's a long shot I know." Dance shoes with their soft suede bottoms were never worn outside. The street and grass would cause undo wear and tear. To a dancer, changing shoes became an immediate habit before going outdoors.

The parking ramp was not too terribly tall. It was one of the first ramps build in the downtown area, so it was only three stories high. It was sandwiched between two taller historic brick building that now housed offices. Most of the ramp occupants were employees who parked there every day. Every day in the same spot - coming at the same time, and leaving at the same time. Edward always took the spot near the back door right up the sloping ramp from the pay booth. Ken, the parking attendant was always there – night or day. He knew everyone and everyone knew him. Edward trusted Ken to watch that big old Caddy from his post. Who knew if Ken spotted everything or everyone, but it was worth the time to ask.

Sydney popped up to the window. Ken was pouring over a book. Without even looking up from his page, Ken droned "What do you want?"

"I suppose the police have been here already about Edward's death." Ken nodded again not lifting his head to make eye contact. "I was just wondering if you saw anything that night." Sydney thought it best to start out with a general question so as not to raise Ken's suspicion as to her real question.

"Nope."

"Was Edward's car parked here that night?" she continued.

"As always." Ken scratched his scruffy beard.

"Did you see anyone come in this back door? Or any car leave around that time?"

"Nope."

"Thanks." Sydney started to turn back to the ramp.

"Of course I wouldn't tell anyone if I did," he stated looking up to make eye contact for the first time.

"He knows," Sydney whispered with a grin. He won't tell me but he knows the answer is in this parking ramp, she thought walking back toward the parked cars. Several of the cars she recognized as vehicles from staff and students. She carefully walked around each paying close attention to the front of the car – the bumper, grill, and lights. If a car hit a person there would be some type of dent or mark. It also might be something so slight that it hadn't been repaired yet. It took her most of her break hour to walk around the dark and chilly cement structure, but nothing appeared unusual or out of the ordinary. Again she told herself there was something that was important in this parking ramp. But what was it? Maybe it wasn't the car at all. Maybe it was something entirely different. Ken wasn't talking, but maybe he would later if she asked the right question. What was the right question?

Walking inside, Antoine was still sitting at the table. She walked across the dance floor and stood in front of him. "OK Antoine. I know that Ken knows something about that night. But what does he know? What is the right question?"

Antoine looked puzzled. "The right question?"

"Yes, what is the right question?" Then she walked back to the teachers' office to change her shoes and think about the question. She hoped she had been right to trust Antoine with her observations after all, he did own a car. Was he the one?

III.

Daniel Loggerman was not happy with Sheila's news about moving out of the apartment. He sat moodily in the back room stretching his long legs out in front of him and leaning back into a folding chair in the corner.

"So she's just leaving you high and dry," Megan was chiding him. "Figures."

Daniel starred into the air without answering her. She knew the answer well enough without him saying one word in response.

"What are you going to do?" she continued pacing the floor and occasionally poking her face in his direction waiting for him to say anything. But he was silent.

"Well you sure can't afford that rent on what you make here. Maybe you'll have to get another part time job. Even that might not make it. Let me suggest something. Why not get another roommate? That's it." She lifted a finger as if coming up with a bright idea on the spur of the moment – which it certainly hadn't been. "Why not find someone else to share the rent with you? But who? Who would understand the horrible hours you keep with a job like this?" Megan continued to pace and look over at the pondering figure in the corner.

Daniel smiled. She had cleverly opened his mind to her intended pathway. His thoughts began to churn. It took a moment before he asked her if she knew anyone who needed a roommate or an apartment.

"You know, I can't say I really know anyone right off the top of my head. But how much did you say the rent was split?" Megan stopped her pacing and stood casually in front of him.

"Well the rent is pretty reasonable only $250 per month without utilities. So split that would be only $125 each. It's a two bedroom duplex. I have the upper, and I guess now Sheila and Morgan have the lower. It's right on the bus line to the studio, so it's pretty convenient. We share a garage. Not that anyone actually has a car. Know anyone who would want such a palace?" Daniel thought he had done well to describe an ideal situation. Fortunately for him, there was someone who already had that same idea before he even described the place.

"Well, I have been to your apartment already with Joan. It is a rather nice duplex. I live alone in efficiency, and it can get pretty claustrophobic at times. Also pretty lonely. I might consider moving in with you, if you really need a roommate..." Daniel had played nicely into Megan's trap.

"You would? That would be great. When do you want to move in?"

"Well I have a month by month lease." Megan had conveniently forgotten to tell him that she had been given notice two weeks ago and had to be out by the end of this month. "I might be able to move a few things in right away. I have accumulated some things – furniture, clothes and of course my hats. So it might take a while to get everything over to your – oops! our place – but I could start the process right away. When can I get a set of keys?" Her smile spread across her face. Daniel looked relieved and didn't seem to notice her pushy nature in the whole matter.

"Maybe I can ask Antoine to help with his car…" Megan didn't wait for an answer and began to talk to herself as she left the room to look for Antoine.

"Smooth. That was very smooth." Sydney sitting in the corner nodded at Daniel.

"Thanks," he grinned.

I didn't mean you, Sydney thought as she smiled back at him. Megan can maneuver things any way she wants. Sydney thought back to the incident at the convention when she convinced Sheila to do her cheer. Why would anyone do something so humiliating? Why was it that Megan could talk someone into doing something so foreign to their nature? Was Megan the kind of person who could have maneuvered Edward Garrett into doing something he didn't want to do? Or was Edward just someone Megan had no interest in manipulating. Maybe Megan had convinced someone else to murder Edward. Did she have the power? It seemed so.

Everyone seemed caught up in the "big move". Megan had conscripted a team to haul and unpack all of her belongings into the unusually messy apartment occupied by Daniel Loggerman. Megan's initial reaction had been a bit shocked as she carried her first item up the outside stairs into the apartment. Her frown as she looked around was noticeable. But she managed to keep a tiny smile as she looked over the possibilities of the place. Daniel didn't seem to be much help. He didn't lift a finger to pick up the scattered pieces of clothing or dirty dishes strewn around the living room area. In fact he announced that he had "things to do" so would have to leave. He scampered out the door and climbed into a car that pulled up to the curb outside. He didn't reappear until the next day at the studio.

Megan took the whole incident in stride and by the time she had to get back to studio herself, she had managed to clean up and move all her belongings into the tiny bedroom formerly occupied by Sheila. She had even managed to clean up the living room tossing much of the mess directly into Daniel's bedroom. Not that he would notice as the rest of his bedroom looked much like the living room had. She scrubbed the kitchen and washed the dirty dishes. It was quite presentable by the time she hopped on the bus the next day.

Sheila on the other hand came into the studio with a new vitality. She seemed quite happy to be out of her former apartment and in with Morgan Canfield. A new atmosphere seemed to do wonders with her disposition. She had even managed to take her fluffy green tutu looking ball gown out of the studio. Maybe now it seemed safe again – not only for her and her cherished possession but also for the rest of the staff who had spent weeks leaping over the thing plopped in the middle of the back teachers' office. Things seemed to have calmed. People were moved around – into better situations – and Edward Garrett's death was becoming a forgotten memory. The main word on everyone's lips was now "Showcase".

Twice a year the studio held a Showcase – a time students were able to perform for others. They spent weeks working on choreographed routines with their teachers, planning elaborate costumes, and inviting family and friends. The event was held in a hotel ballroom complete with a nationally known judge or dance couple as guests. The main concern in the weeks prior to the Showcase was preparation of the performance routines. Scheduling more lesson times and working on a selected dance to just the right piece of music became the focus. Teachers would come in early and stay late to have another staff person help them play with certain amalgamations and count out just the right number of measures for a sequence. It called for teamwork and creativity.

Antoine casually walked out to the dance floor to observe Daniel's lesson with Gwen Blake. Gwen was not a particularly talented dancer yet – of course she was just a beginner who was taking only one lesson a week. But she was young and beautiful. That always made a nice dance partnership - both tall and good looking. Gwen was giggling over something. Her white blond hair bounced with each back and forth secret whispered between the two of them.

"So Miss Blake, what will you be doing for Showcase?" Antoine interrupted.

"I have been asking her that very question," Daniel immediately fired back at Antoine.

"You have?" Gwen looked at Daniel from under heavy black eyelashes. "I don't recall…".

Quickly Daniel broke in. "Yes we have been considering a Rumba."

"The dance of romance," Antoine commented with a nod. "Sexy and sultry. I would say that would be a perfect choice for the two of you."

"The dance of romance? Why that sounds just perfect. What do I have to do?" Gwen fanned her gaze to Daniel's face.

Daniel explained what a Showcase was in excellent terminology as if he had told her the same thing over and over again which clearly he hadn't. Antoine waited for her response, and she didn't disappoint. "When do we start?" she quipped.

Antoine rolled his eyes. Only Daniel noticed as Gwen was staring quite intently into Daniel's eyes with a coy and demure expression. "Right away!" Daniel announced cheerily and plastered a convincing grin across face. "Ooh," Gwen cooed.

Antoine walked calmly off the floor and reached the reception desk to take in a deep breath and explode in anger. He ranted for a short time to Morgan about Daniel not doing his job and always having to follow up to make sure information was given to his students. Then just as quickly as he had vented his anger, he put a crisp smile on his face as a group of students eagerly entered the front door slinging their coats and shoe bags in the direction of the rack in the corner. Cheerfully he greeted each one with encouraging remarks about the progress of their Showcase routines.

"Ok", Daniel exploded into the back teachers' office. "I need a Rumba. Quickly. Help." Megan turned her head and ignored his request, but Sydney limply rose from her seat and followed him out to the dance floor to begin some suggestions for easy Rumba patterns for Gwen Blake. As each piece of music played Sydney would quip, "This is a nice Rumba." Finally Daniel chose one that was contemporary and easy to listen to. "Nice beat," Sydney agreed. They put together an entrance which consisted of some walks forward in a shadow position into a lady's turn, walks around the back of the man as he did some second position breaks.

"She'll like this," Daniel agreed as Sydney showed him how Gwen could caress his cheek as she walked around past him, behind his back and to the front for a long and low dip before beginning the middle of the routine. They put in some fifth positions and a cross over with a turn. Sydney suggested a passing box step that Damian Vito had demonstrated at the Convention. Daniel of course hadn't been at that dance session, so he liked the new way to amalgamate the basic Rumba step. She showed him another over the head arm change that Damian had done with the basic. It was sleek and sensual.

"And for the end position," Sydney was saying, "how about this leg wrap for Gwen with this dip across the body."

"Oh, I like that," Daniel complimented. "Let's try that again."

Kerri Blake had been out for the first part of the day at a photo shoot and was just arriving. She walked into the ballroom and watched briefly. Without so much as a nod of the head, she sauntered off down the hall with a totally blank expression on her face.

Daniel watched her leave with a slight look of concern on his face. "Don't mind her," Sydney commented. "She'll love the routine once she sees you and Gwen heat up the floor." Daniel nodded, and they danced through the whole amalgamation again.

"I'd stay away from Daniel Loggerman if I were you," Kerri Blake hissed as Sydney bounded into the back room to change her shoes and grab her programs.

"What are you talking about?" Sydney quickly searched through the programs piled on her desk.

"Just what I said," Kerri repeated. "Stay away from Daniel."

"You mean out there on the dance floor? We were choreographing your sister Gwen's showcase routine."

"Oh." Suddenly Kerri's intonation changed. "I'm sorry. You say that was for Gwen?"

"Yup. A hot, steamy Rumba. No one will ever guess Daniel is gay," Sydney stacked her lesson books up and turned to leave. She didn't notice the expression on Kerri Blake's face – a stony cold look that simmered with renewed anger.

IV.

Suzanna stood at the front desk checking out the financial reports as Sheila and Morgan scampered in together chattering away. A wisp of chill breeze clung to their coats.

"I could get used to this ride situation. Thanks for the lift," Sheila was saying in a dragged out drawl.

"Your welcome," Morgan retorted back taking off her coat and hat.

Although it was early in the day and the normal schedule wasn't to start for another half hour, there were couples already out on the floor in the middle of lessons. With the Showcase quickly approaching, the teachers scheduled extra lesson times in the mornings. The music was louder than usual and the four couples on the floor had already staked out their little territories. Carson Hunter and Miss Witherspoon, an elderly woman who enjoyed her dance lessons for as long as the studio had been in existence, were back in the far corner working on a Waltz. The white hair piled on top of her head made her appear taller. Her slight frame was elegantly dressed in a royal blue shirt waist dress with a full skirt to "better Waltz in" – as she would always answer to a compliment on her appearance. The wrinkles on her face were more like valleys but hardly noticeable because of her young, youthful spirit.

Sydney Monroe and her student Mr. Lindsey were in the opposite corner working on Cha Cha. Mr. Lindsey was thin and not any taller than Miss Monroe. Always laughing throughout his lesson, he brought a cheerful atmosphere to the entire room whenever he had a lesson.

Anna Smith and her couple, the Springers, were concentrating on a very advanced Tango in the center of the floor while Daniel and Gwen Blake were trying to avoid everyone with their Rumba. They would start an amalgamation and then move to a different patch of the floor as the Springers would sweep across the floor to within inches of them. This gradual migration became a pattern until Gwen and Daniel were almost dancing on the tables alongside the windowed wall. The Springers were an older couple who were considered "Silver" dancers – more than simply social dancers; they trained in advanced dance techniques that made them a favorite couple to watch. They did not, however, pay much attention to anyone else on the floor and would monopolize the space creating treacherous conditions for anyone else trying to dance. Bulldozers might be a term used for the Springers.

Carson put Miss Witherspoon in her starting spot and scurried across the floor to put their Waltz music on. Miss Witherspoon held her starting pose and waited for him to hurry back to her side to begin their introduction. The other couples moved quietly to the edge of the floor and watched as they danced through the routine. Every so often the teachers watching would clap, and Miss Witherspoon would lift her chin elegantly acknowledging the praise. Suzanna stood in the corner and observed everyone. She clapped and nodded as the couple finished their dance with a flourish. Miss Witherspoon curtseyed and smiled with pleasure at the added attention.

"Oh, that will look lovely!" Suzanna beamed as she went over to help them smooth out some of the spots that hadn't moved as well as they could have.

The noon time sun streamed in through the windows and the sheer curtains. Sydney walked Mr. Lindsey to the front desk and asked Morgan to schedule another morning appointment.

"What day would be good for you?" Morgan asked tapping the pencil and paging through the large appointment sheets clipped to the slanted board in front of her.

Sydney decided to quickly run to the corner deli for a sandwich before dance session. She scooted out the back door thinking she would take a look around the parking lot again on the way to the store. Parked up along the ramp were a number of cars she hadn't seen before. Students most likely, she thought. She slowly walked around some of the vehicles that she didn't recognize. There was a large beige Oldsmobile with streaks of rust along the side by the doors. She checked out the front and noticed some dents around the front lights. She paused to take a closer look. This certainly was caused by hitting something – or someone – but the car was so old, it might have been dented for some time now. She copied down the license plate number with the intent to ask Ken later who owned this car.

Then she spotted a little red compact that was also not there when she looked before. She circled to the front of this one as well. It was new, yet had a small patch that appeared to be repainted. The spot was slightly different than the rest of the car. She also copied this number down then hurried along to pick up her lunch, tucking the scrap of paper into her pocket. Her mind went to egg salad on wheat.

The day continued through the dance session, meeting and further lessons. At the end of the day, the staff stayed to run over their routine for the Showcase. This year, they would perform the multi-dance routine Suzanna had choreographed for the Convention. It would make matters so much better to have something they all knew and could simply brush up on for a few moments each evening. Everyone was so busy with all the student routines, that the decision to show a routine they had already performed was a welcome relief. The staff was scattered throughout the ballroom taking advantage of the time to rest while several were finishing up their lessons. Sheila skipped in with a lightness she had never shown before. Suddenly, she struck a pose and belted out loudly, "I'm Sheila Pickford from Minneapolis and all I have to say is E-I-E-I-O!" It was so unexpected that everyone stared for a moment and then burst out into laughter. Sheila continued to prance around the room past Megan Meeker who was initially red with embarrassment but then joined in with a chuckle.

"You seem to be feeling pretty good tonight," Suzanna said brightly.

"I am. I am feeling good. In fact I feel better than I have ever felt since coming to this studio." Sheila drawled,

"It's amazing what a little change of scenery will do for a person."

Megan slumped into a chair in the corner. Daniel Loggerman was not yet in the room. So any reference to their previous living situation was only an insinuation caught by a few.

"Let's rehearse!" Sheila prompted with a light nonchalant air and a wave of her hand. And they did. They rehearsed for the first time with no tension and no glares across the room. It was the most pleasant hour the studio had experienced since Edward Garrett's death – no, rather from the moment Sheila Pickford had first stepped through the studio door before Edward's death.

Morgan waited to give Sheila a ride home, doing paperwork as they rehearsed. As she put her coat on and rechecked the schedule for the next day, Sydney Monroe, weighed down with clothes and a bag, struggled to carry her load to the waiting room. She fished awkwardly for some semblance of organization and dropped the slip of paper from her pocket.

"What's this?" Morgan reached down to pick up the paper and help her sling her arm into her coat sleeve.

"Those are car license plate numbers. I'm trying to see if any of the cars in the ramp have front damage. You know like someone hit something – like a person," Sydney explained.

"Well, this number is my license plate." Morgan pointed to the first number on the page.

"That old beige boat out by the door?"

"That would be the one. That would be my boat." Morgan sniffed as if insulted that she might be considered a suspect.

"Good! That eliminates one of them. Now all I have to do is find the owner of the second one." Sydney tried not to sound accusing. "I'm sorry. I just thought that anyone who hit Edward might have some damage to their car. There are so many here at the studio who don't drive or own cars, that it seemed a good idea to check out some of the cars in the ramp. I don't mean to point any fingers. I'm just doing a bit of sleuthing on my own. There doesn't seem to be anything happening to find the killer and who knows, the killer might be right here in the studio working side by side with us every day."

"I see what you mean," Morgan pondered. "It would be nice to solve this thing once and for all. I hadn't thought about the possibility that someone we know might have killed Edward. But I guess it would have to be someone connected to the studio somehow. What can I do to help you?"

Sydney chuckled. "Well, you could help me find the owner of this car. It might not even be relevant, but then again it could be a clue."

"Ok, I'll check with Ken when I leave. What does the car look like?"

"Red. Small compact. I'm not that great with makes and models," Sydney confessed. "But you can copy down the number of the license to show him. I'm sure he'll know by the license who owns it."

V.

In spite of the clamor involved with the upcoming Showcase, Sydney was determined to get to the studio early for the exercise class with the hope of finding out any new information from Morgan about the car's owner. Throughout the exercise session she was mildly distracted as she positioned herself on the floor with an eye on the front door so she could excuse herself when Morgan arrived for a private chat at the desk. But a watched door never seems to open and that is just what happened that morning. The door never opened, and Morgan Canfield never showed.

All through dance session and meeting time, Morgan was noticeable absent. When Sydney asked Sheila about Morgan, she vaguely mentioned she thought Morgan was sick. Sydney's mind began to churn and it moved from possibility to possibility throughout her daily lessons.

"What seems to be bothering you today?" one student asked when Sydney didn't respond to a question he asked.

"Nothing. Sorry, what was that again?"

OK. So what if she had been wrong, and Morgan was in fact the murderer of Edward Garrett. What if the evidence on her car was just that – evidence of a hit and run? What if Morgan panicked and simply left, leaving Sydney with little more than a theory? Or on the other hand, what if Morgan had discovered the owner of the little red car from Ken, and it was indeed the killer. What if that killer had done something to Morgan so no one else would discover the truth? Or maybe Morgan was too afraid to face that person and was hiding.

Sydney's mind began to move from theory to theory until she began to feel very confused and very nervous. She went home that evening looking over her shoulder and carefully locking her doors. It could very well be any of the possibilities she imagined. She would wait cautiously until the next day to see if Morgan came in and scattered to the wind all of her nice little fears.

But the next day was the same. Morgan Canfield never showed up for work. Sheila was once again just as vague about Morgan's whereabouts. This time Sydney wasn't ready to let it go. On her lunch hour she convinced Antoine they needed to go over to Morgan's apartment to check on her. Antoine had his car at the studio that day and was her only viable means of transportation to the duplex Morgan and Sheila were sharing with Daniel and Megan. A bus trip would be too time consuming during a lunch hour.

Unfortunately, the studio lunch hours were never during a true "lunch hour" and the business community working in the downtown area was just leaving work for the day. The trip was frustrating and long in spite of the car and the relatively short distance to their destination.

Arriving at the older house now divided into an upper apartment and a lower level, Sydney stopped to gaze at the classic white two story with its blue shudders and front porch. It was the corner house nestled into an older neighborhood that many upper middle class moved away from - choosing the newer suburbs instead. Once a nice little neighborhood filled with families and kids at the nearby park, it was now becoming filled instead with short term renters or older couples who didn't have the finances or the motivation to leave.

She and Antoine went to the front door and rang the bell. They waited and rang again. Now Sydney was really beginning to panic. Should they call the police? Was Morgan even there – in distress and needing help from some unknown assailant – or was she gone? Had she run.

In one final attempt, Sydney pulled back her fist to pound on the door with extra force, but with a sudden jerk, the door opened almost sending her sprawling across the threshold.

"What in God's name do you two want?" Morgan was in slippers and robe with a dripping nose and a fist full of tissues. Her eyes looked like puffy slits, and her expression was anything but delighted to have company.

"Thank God, you are all right," Sydney breathed a sigh.

"Alright? Alright? I don't think so. Didn't Sheila tell you I was sick? I haven't felt this bad since … since never! I've never felt this bad. With the Showcase coming up I didn't want all of you to get sick, but I guess you thwarted that. I hope you don't get this. No. I take that back. I hope you do get this so you can feel just as miserable especially after making me get out of bed to come out to answer this door. Now leave me alone!" She slammed the door, and the click of the lock could clearly be heard.

Antoine and Sydney stood for a moment on the front porch just taking in the whole scenario and staring for a moment at each other. "Well, back to the good old world of rush hour traffic," Antoine announced and turned to go back to the car. Sydney followed skulking along behind. All that worry for nothing.

VI.

It was Sunday and Morgan Canfield did not attend the Showcase. Sydney had a friend drive her downtown to the Danforth Hotel early that morning. Sunday mornings were unusually quiet in downtown Minneapolis. No businesses open, few buses running, and no people in suits scurrying about with briefcases. The sky was hazy with clouds. Not exactly dark and dreary, but the lack of sun certainly felt gloomy. Sydney jumped out with a quick "thank you" carrying a duffle bag and a fist full of costumes on hangers covered with a large garbage bag – the poor man's suit bag. She scuttled in through the revolving door asking at the front desk where the dance event was to be held. After dropping off her bags in the staff dressing room – a long narrow non-descript room with a clothing rack in the center of the floor and a few well placed mirrors – she ambled into the ballroom.

Several men in starched white jackets were putting together the parquet dance floor. Others were carefully covering round tables with white table clothes. Chandeliers lit up the room giving an elegant soft atmosphere. The carpet was an industrial pattern in a calming gray and black tone.

Sydney was always the first at any event. It just didn't feel right not to get there, settle in and feel relaxed when everything started. Unlike Edward Garrett who was always late to everything. It had become the studio joke when asked what time something started was to ask if it was "real time" or "studio time". "Studio time" referred to Edward's habit of arriving two sometimes three hours late to anything. It got to be such a problem that sometimes they would tell him an event started at 1:00 if it really started at 3:00. That way he would only arrive an hour later than expected. He even banned clocks from the studio so students wouldn't know if their lessons started late. They used an egg timer instead to note the length of each lesson. It worked as long as the desk staff remembered to set it as the beginning of each hour.

Because Sydney was always early, the hotel staff always assumed she was "in charge". It would seem the first to arrive would be the one most interested in making sure the event was running smoothly in its preparation. So they of course they asked her how she like the placement of the dance floor. She stood back and acted as if she were pondering the question before nodding her approval. They would always sigh in relief and smile as they kept pushing the squares of wood into place.

Some of the students had stayed in the hotel over night and were filtering down for a cup of coffee or a peek at the place they would be dancing. Sydney quickly slid into the staff room to put on a dress and check her makeup. She always felt it important to look professional when dealing with students. It was her job.

The studio staff was scheduled to rehearse promptly at 10:00 for half an hour before students could officially arrive to practice routines on the floor. The hotel floor always took some time to get used to because it was pieces of wood with gaps between squares that never quite fit properly. Heels sometimes got caught or the direction of the room made orientation seem off somehow.

The rehearsal of course started late. They walked through their routine without music to get placements and then by the time that was done, the music sound system was set up and ready for their routine record that skipped. Students began to congregate outside the heavy ballroom doors now closed to keep the rehearsal and sound checks more private. A table at the end of the room had freshly brewing coffee and pitchers of ice water. It began to feel warm and more comfortable with the morning aromas filling the formerly stuffy space. Joan Ericson was putting centerpieces and bowls of mints at each table. She scattered a few neat program booklets as well. Everyone was waking up and feeling the excitement of the day they spent weeks in preparation for. Soon the doors opened and the students already dressed in their dance dresses and tuxedos entered to the sound of a background waltz. Some had on the glitter and dark eye shadow of evening make up. Others sported dresses with feathers and sequined bodices. Couples began to discuss their position on the floor and where the judges would be seated. Another hour and the event would be off to a rousing start.

For some the day was one brief moment in the spot light showcasing a routine they had spent hours learning and hopefully perfecting – finished in a minute or two. For others it was many, many routines. This was true for several of the teachers. Anna Smith had over thirty routines with students, and Carson danced over fifty times. Sometimes Sydney would see Carson sitting in the staff room shaking out his arms and nursing a cool glass of ice water. The male teachers complained mostly about the pain in their arms from holding up their partners' dance frame. The women instead found the pain to be in their feet, alternating their heeled dance shoes frequently to give a little change and hopefully an added relief.

The dance judges today were Henri and Claire Burmeister from New York City. They were champion dancers in the theater arts division and would present a spectacular show that evening along with the staff routine. Claire sat at the head table with a platinum blond head of hair draped around her shoulders. Tonight it would be tightly wound in a hairdo plastered to her head. Today she looked fairly normal. She was dressed in a conservative navy suit and tall closed toed dress shoes to match. Henri was in a navy suit as well. No matter, they would stand out from the rest of the dancers and staff as perfect professionals. Their bright white pearly teeth sparkled along with their perfect upright posture and all knowing expressions. They smiled at each routine and nodded politely at each conclusion. Each student left the floor in giddiness with the impression that Henri and Claire approved.

At the conclusion of the student portion of the showcase, everyone exited the ballroom to congregate in the bar or maybe go up to their room to change clothes for the evening's events – dinner, awards and the show.

Sydney and Carson remained in the ballroom. Carson carried glasses of white wine to the judges table as the hotel crew hurried to clean the ballroom, reset the tables and prepare for the dinner to be served in an hour. Each showcase was the same. Sydney and Carson would tabulate the scores. Henri and Claire had given each dancer a comment sheet and a score. Of course old Mr. Ganfield wouldn't be in the same event category as young Miss Clark, so it was their job to put each score sheet in the proper pile and from there determine who had indeed won first, second and third place. The teachers would also compete, winning points for good student scores. The most enjoyable part about this tabulation duty was the opportunity to watch Henri and Claire rehearse for their evening performance. No longer dressed in their navy suits, Claire and Henri were in warm up suits and tights. Now they could determine where the chandeliers would prevent them from doing a particular lift and where they would have to move on the floor to do a drop that didn't hit the crack in the parquet floor. It was now the time for Sydney and Carson to relax and for Henri and Claire to fret. Not that anything they did wouldn't seem perfect to the audience. They were used to the "oohs" and "aahs" that came with a spectacular lift high into the air. They also knew it was dangerous no matter how many times they had successfully completed the move, there was always that one time that it might not work. Life was a gamble and dancing was always a risk.

The dinner – the usual hotel chicken and vegetables – was a success. After a long day of dancing, the nerves, and the drinks after, a warm meal was always a delight. Dessert was a choice of chocolate parfait or apple cobbler. Then of course the pot of coffee was placed on the table and the dishes cleared. Suzanna Caldwell welcomed everyone and invited them to dance as the music played combinations of Rumbas and Fox Trots. After a few dances, she asked everyone to be seated for the announcing of the awards. Everyone clapped briskly as each accepted an award and the flash of the camera captured each student and teacher with the judges. This time, Claire was dressed elegantly in a stunning pale pink chiffon gown and Henri had on a tuxedo with an unusually subtle patterned cummerbund and matching bowtie. They were a tiny couple perfectly matching in height and slenderness.

The music played a few more songs allowing the staff to change for their routine. When Suzanna announced the staff and they began their routine, the crowd wildly applauded. The routine was a success and Suzanna sat with a hint of a smile on her lips. She had done what Edward always told her she couldn't. It felt so good. It was too bad he hadn't been there to see it. The success was a bit bittersweet.

The lights dimmed again, and Clair snaked through the crowd in a flowing black cape. Her hair now piled on her head accented her feathery false eyelashes and glistening red lips. Henri following in a black form fitting cat suit pulling off her cape to reveal a black mini dress cut down the back and criss crossed with sequins. The music blared and they began to dance, spinning around the floor and in and out of high throws and low drips. The crowd gasped and clapped drawing in deep breaths of excitement that any human being could really do such amazing feats. They finished with a high lift and a sudden drop from Claire into Henri's arms. It was over. The night was through.

The staff formed a receiving line to say a final good – by to all of the students. The energy was gradually lowering to exhaustion. Sydney packed up her bag and costumes. She would hitch a ride with Carson. Carson who almost never drove anywhere lived only a block from Sydney. His beat up old station wagon usually sat quietly at his curb, as he preferred to take the more convenient bus to and from work.

They slowly walked out to the parking ramp that the hotel provided for their guests. It was small but free with an event stamp on the parking ticket. The ramp was quiet and dark. Carson looked around to remember where he had parked and finally directed Sydney toward the second level of the ramp. They slunk past mostly empty stalls until they spotted the station wagon up ahead – right next to the small red compact. The one Sydney was interested in. She quickly made note of the spot she had viewed the other evening – the discoloration from a newly painted patch on the front hood. It was there. She looked around for the owner, but there was no one in sight. Someone from the studio owned this car - someone who was at the Showcase that day. No longer comfortable to share her speculations with anyone after the past few days lamenting about Morgan and her noted absence, she didn't tell Carson about her suspicions. Home and a comfortable warm bed were waiting.

VII.

Suzanna Caldwell smiled. Today would be busy as would the next day. The Burmeisters stayed on an extra few days to go over comments and results with the students who had performed at the Showcase. They would also make suggestions for future routines and teach the staff dance sessions.

"You know it's a shame not to use Edward's office for all of the conferences with students today," Joan Ericson commented.

"Oh, I don't know. It wouldn't feel right..." Suzanna hesitated.

"He's dead. He's not using it," Joan said flatly. "Besides, it's the only nice place we have to meet with students. You certainly can't use the dance floor or the back office. It's perfect!"

"You're right, of course," Suzanna smiled. "I've always wanted to fling back that heavy curtain and look out on the dance floor. After all, that's why he designed the window overlooking the floor. Why he never used it, I can't say. It always seemed a waste of its intended purpose."

She walked slowly over to the door and opened it as if opening a sacred vault. Flipping on the light switch, she looked over the dark cherry desk and the primitive artwork that graced the walls. Edward was fond of art from the Caribbean so had native masks and colorful abstract paintings giving the room a finished look that was missing from the other areas of the studio. She pulled the heavy drapes opened and let the light from the ballroom flood the area. It seemed spectacular - no longer dreary and cold. Everything on the desk was neat and tidy. Nothing seemed out of place. She carefully took some of the personal photos and knickknacks from the top of the desk and the book shelf placing them into the almost empty drawers. She felt more comfortable without the reminders of Edward Garrett. Settling in at his desk, she adjusted the overstuffed desk chair for her smaller stature and scoped the area. Edward had an expensive desk set with a leather trimmed pad and gold pen set. It was beautiful. She fingered the pen and slowly caressed the top of the leather. It felt too thick – a bit lumpy. She lifted the pad and pulled out an envelope. It was sealed with a wax impressed stamp and marked with a flowing handwriting "Last Will and Testimony".

"Oh, my God!" Suzanna gasped. She held the envelope and began to breathe deeply. "Joan, come here!"

They both stared intently at the envelope. "What should we do?" Suzanna whispered.

"I think we need to call the police," Joan walked quietly out to the front desk and made the call. And that was that.

Henri and Claire had been escorted from their hotel by Antoine. They looked crisp and dapper – Henri in a navy pin striped suit, a starched white shirt with a narrow navy tie and Claire in a cream pants suit trimmed in gold buttons and braid. Her blond hair was swept up into a tight bun with a gold crocheted net. They both smiled politely and sat down in Edward's office with Suzanna to go over the schedule for the day. Each student performing in the Showcase was scheduled for a special lesson with the judges to go over comments on the performance and suggestions for the future. Suzanna organized the pile of score sheets and reminded the couple who each dancer was and what they had performed.

"She was the one who did the cha cha in the sparkling pink short dress…".

"Oh, yes. She had a nice cross over break and very nice feet on her turns," Claire would comment to Henri who would nod. He would then take down a note on a pad to refer to during the lesson.

The lessons would begin early at 11 AM and were arranged for half hour time slots in order to accommodate everyone. The other staff members were encouraged to observe the critiques to glean as much dance knowledge as possible from the best of the best. Then the teacher and student would go into Edward's office to discuss the comments and arrange any further additions to their dance program if it was warranted. Claire and Henri would be willing to do some special choreography for students who were interested in beginning a new routine for a future competition or showcase.

The day went smoothly, and Claire and Henri taught an excellent dance lesson first to the students during their usual group lesson time and later at the end of the day to the staff. They worked on partner connections and techniques in leading and following.

The next day would be more of the same. This time Claire came in wearing a bright red short dress with matching red satin dance shoes. She wore her hair down around her shoulders. Henri was in a pale gray suit, pin striped gray shirt and a charcoal gray bow tie. The schedule again began early at 11 AM. with two of Carson's students.

The first was a middle aged woman who had danced for a number of years. She had performed a Tango at the Showcase. Claire commented on her dramatic performance and the nice flare she showed for the traditional Tango fans and dips. They worked on a few footwork changes in her introductory sequence and suggested a closer body position when dancing the Tango. Then Henri mentioned an elegant Waltz for her next routine, commenting on the possibility of using some of the body contact exercises used in her Tango to put some advanced technique into the Waltz. He and Claire demonstrated an amalgamation of three patterns that involved a twinkle with syncopated under arm turn into an oversway. Claire's head position, tilted back and away from Henri shifted elegantly as he brought her around from the beginning of the twinkle into her turn and then back out to her dip. Carson led his student through the patterns and listened as Claire suggested an arm exercise to use for added grace in their linework during the turn. Suzanna observing the lesson wrote some notes and took the woman into the office to discuss ideas for doing the Waltz along with adding to her Tango.

The second of Carson's students was a younger woman who worked as a waitress at night and came in during the afternoons for her lessons. She was a fairly new student and had performed a Latin Merengue at the Showcase. Henri began by working on adding Cuban hip motion to her entire routine. Patterns are often easier to teach while the technique of actually doing a step using the body is typically more difficult. This was the case here. The hip motion was challenging and yet gave an authenticity to her movement. Claire suggested they might try using the hip motion exercises in her other dances particularly the Rumba which is slower and sometimes easier to incorporate body motion into the basic patterns. Other staff members took note of the way Claire and Henri had the student use her feet and legs to develop the motion in her hips. They began to try some of the techniques with each other, nodding agreement at the effectiveness of the method.

Joan had gone out to bring back a quick snack for Claire and Henri. They sat at a glass table eating tiny sandwich samples from the deli at the corner and sipping orange flavored tea. The staff had scattered for a few moments of break time before the dance session. Today Henri had promised a few new patterns in the cha cha that could be used in routines choreographed for their students. New variations were always fun to try. The hour went by quickly. Then Henri led a discussion on teaching techniques and presentation methods for more advanced material.

At 3:00 Gwen Blake sat in the waiting area ready for her lesson with the pair. Daniel Loggerman rushed back to the teachers' office to prepare her lesson plan and grab her routine music.

"My, but you are a lovely couple," Claire began as Gwen and Daniel got into dance position for a warm up dance. Gwen blushed and fluttered her eyelashes at Daniel. "As I watched your Rumba," she continued, "I couldn't help but think how nice you two look together. Both so tall and slender. I know that Henri and I, as short as we are also find we are well suited for each other. We seem to match, and that works well out on the floor when we dance together. The same can be said for you." Henri nodded his agreement.

"The Rumba is a very romantic dance," Claire grabbed Henri's hand and began to dance a basic box step. She added a slight smile at her partner who slyly smiled back. "It's almost as if you are viewing a secret when you watch a Rumba – a romance that hasn't yet become public knowledge. It makes you feel intimate with people you hardly know just by watching how they react to each other during their dance."

Claire and Henri moved from the basic into some turns and open breaks. "I don't know, can you feel that when you watch Henri and I do our Rumba?" Claire asked as Henri led her to under his arm to face Gwen and Daniel.

Gwen stared without saying anything for a moment. She thought hard about what Claire had said and slowly nodded her head. "Yes, I can feel it."

Claire moved away from Henri and grasped Daniel's hand leading him to dance the Rumba with her. For a brief moment, Gwen's eyes flashed in anger. But that anger only showed for a second, and no one in the room was watching her – they all had their eyes on Claire and Daniel doing a Rumba with Cuban hip motion and a sensual upper body follow through that caused the still room to echo a few intakes of air from those observing. They were deeply feeling the intimate nature of the dance.

"Now you try," Claire stopped abruptly and moved aside motioning to Gwen to take her place in the partnership. Gwen hesitated, but with a slight uneasiness soon took Daniel's hand and began to dance. "Feel your dance," Claire whispered.

"How do you like your dance lessons?" Claire asked at the end of the session. Gwen again blushed and nodded. "Good?" Claire again asked. Gwen nodded looking down at the floor. "Then you need to set higher goals for yourself. You need to challenge your abilities."

Gwen and Daniel walked into the office to meet with Suzanna. "That one is not shy," Claire said softly. "She only pretends to be." Only Henri and Sydney were near enough to hear her comments. Claire's jaw was clenched tight for a moment as she watched the two take their seats in the office, then she turned and smiling went on to the next lesson.

As the evening was coming to a close, Joan with the phone to her ear motioned to Suzanna to come toward the front desk.

"Yes, I understand. Tomorrow? Yes, we will all be here. Thank you." She put down the phone and pulled Suzanna closer. "That was the police about the will. They want to read it at the staff meeting tomorrow. Evidently there are parts that apply to everyone. Make sure each staff member is present without telling them why. OK?" There was a stillness as the two made eye contact. "I wonder why Edward wrote out a will so soon before his death. Do you think he knew what was going to happen?"

The two huddled around the desk didn't notice that Sheila had been standing near by. "I think it might be because of me," she said in a hushed voice.

"What?" Both Suzanna and Joan now noticed Sheila staring up at the ceiling.

"I'm sorry, I didn't mean to eaves drop. I heard you talking about a will. I made a suggestion to Edward a few weeks after I came that he should really think about writing one because there seemed to be so much confusion and chaos in the studio here as to who did what and what belonged to whom. It seemed to make sense that he write down his intentions about the business so nothing would be misconstrued. Then things began to turn around a bit, and I forgot about it. I guess he listened to me after all. Imagine that!" Sheila lowered her eyes and made eye contact with Suzanna. The two were locked in space somehow trying to read the thoughts on the other end of the connection. Suzanna couldn't help but imagine what Sheila had suggested be put in that will. Tomorrow would tell.

The next early afternoon as the teachers gathered in the ballroom for the usual meeting, there was an air of curiosity. They all had been told it was a mandatory meeting, with no other explanation. When the police detective wandered in still wearing his long trench coat, the whispers began. Could they have found Edward's killer? Was there information about the murder?

The detective introduced himself and pulled an envelope from his pocket. "This is the last will and testament written and signed by Edward Garrett. We have had the handwriting analyzed and recognize it to be a genuine document. Without further ado I will read what Edward Garrett's last wishes were."

After a slight murmur from the seated group, he cleared his throat and began to read the two pages. Suzanna was willed the studio and all of Edward's music collection – quite a generous and possibly valuable collection. Edward was in the habit of spending his money on expensive clothing, often traveling to other countries to find just the right items for his wardrobe. When he was tired of something, he would bring it in to the studio one day on a whim and give it an overwhelmed teacher. His closet full of clothes and shoes would be distributed to the male staff. They all grinned at the prospect of some new "old" clothes. Daniel was the only one who would really fit into Edward's long and narrow shoes, so he would accumulate a large new shoe wardrobe. His smile was especially bright.

Each staff member would be able to select a piece from Edward's art collection. He had numerous paintings and sculptures that were mostly contemporary and generally primitive in style. But this bequeath could be of some value if they chose wisely. Kerri Blake was to have a gold ring that she had admired. It had a cluster of diamonds and rubies. The rest of Edward's jewelry and his condo with its furnishings were willed to Amanda. Not much could be said of any monetary assets. It was widely known that Edward usually spent everything he made as soon as he made it – if not before. Oh, yes, the detective added at the end... Gwen Blake was to receive his Cadillac. She had recently gotten her driver's license and could make use of a car.

This last piece of information caused some to look around curiously and raised a few eyebrows. Gwen Blake? That was an odd sentiment. No one even knew that Edward had ever met Gwen formally.

Amanda was seated in the back of the room. She showed no surprise at any of the items listed nor did it seem to surprise her who was mentioned in the will. She came from a wealthy family and had certainly never married Edward for the fortune that he never had. She was satisfied with bits of remembrances of Edward and his often times bizarre life. She intended to go through his condo soon to sort and see what else needed to be donated elsewhere. It was a relief to know that it was indeed hers so it wasn't sitting there waiting to be determined by the courts what would be done with it all.

The most shocked in the whole matter was Suzanna. She had no idea that she would in fact be the sole owner of the studio. She looked around the room with a new eye, imagining what she should do first. She stood and announced, "You've all worked very hard this weekend with the showcase and the lessons with our distinguished judges. So if you have no lessons scheduled today, you may have the day off. I do need someone to volunteer to stay and teach the evening's group lesson however. But the rest of you, take a breather and enjoy the rest of your day."

There was a rustle of excitement. This was a rare occurrence to be given the day off. It was also a rare occurrence to be receiving gifts of art and clothing. Yes, today seemed bright in spite of the crisp, cold cloudy weather outside.

"I will be going over the books with a fine tooth comb," Suzanna announced to Morgan and Joan. "I didn't have much incentive before to really take a good hard look at all the numbers, but suddenly today I do." She smiled, but it was a nervous smile. It really hadn't sunk in yet what she had just received from a man who had made her life miserable most of the time. Joan patted her on the back and congratulated her.

VIII.

Sydney volunteered to stay and teach the evening group. She had a lesson scheduled the hour before anyway, so it was no stretch for her to stay a bit longer. Besides, she had a quiet curiosity she needed help solving. She was hoping Joan or Suzanna would be of some help with that quest. She would normally speak to Morgan at the desk, but somehow she still didn't have the trust back in Morgan that she had when she asked for help with the car identity. And it still wasn't identified. That idea had fallen by the wayside with the chaos of Showcase and the heavily scheduled Monday and Tuesday. Morgan had seemed to avoid talking with her the past few days, and she still wondered why. Had she discovered something she shouldn't have known? She would be careful who she trusted.

Suzanna sat in Edward's – or rather – her office. The large polished desk and the thickly carpeted room seemed to swallow her up, yet she seemed to be quite giddy after the reading of the will. She had on a pair of narrow lens reading glasses held about her neck with a beaded chain and was closely peering at page after page of documents.

"Excuse me," Sydney tapped on the door. "I don't mean to interrupt, but could I have a few words with you?"

Suzanna laid down the paper she was reading and motioned her in. "What can I do for you?"

"I just have a few questions I would like to ask, if I may. It's strictly curiosity and nothing more. I just would like this whole murder thing to come to an end. It seems so stressful to distrust everyone that we work with on a daily basis. One of them has to know more about this than they are saying, and I suspect that one is even the murderer. Doesn't that bother you?" Sydney sunk into the soft chair in front of the desk.

"Yes, it does. Especially now that I'm a little more stable with my future plans. Now that I know I own this studio, I don't have to worry about my job – will I have one, won't I have one? Who will be my boss? It's a big relief and I must say quite surprising. Especially after my conversation with Sheila last night." Suzanna told Sydney about what Sheila had said about encouraging Edward to write the will. She described how she found the will in this very office as she prepared for Claire and Henri's visit.

Sydney listened carefully and then mentioned that Claire had said something that made her wonder about something. She was even more curious as to what she had meant after the will presented Gwen Blake with Edward's car. Suzanna nodded. She agreed that it did seem strange, but she was so shocked by the announcement that the studio belonged to her that she hadn't listened as closely to the remaining will as she should have.

"What do you know about Gwen Blake?" Sydney asked.

"Well, I know of course that she is Kerri's younger sister. I don't think that she is even as old as she appears. Her tall thin model appearance makes her look more mature." Suzanna thought for a moment. "I know their mother is dead and their father is very wealthy – he owns the Blake Hotel. It was passed on down in the family from his father, so that means the family comes from money. They don't seem to want for much."

"Exactly! If they are so wealthy, why would Edward will an old Cadillac to Gwen? I mean, it's a nice car and everything, but it's just that – an old car. Her father could easily buy her any kind of car she wants. I would think an expensive sports car would fit more with her personality. She seems like one who would want the latest and most fashionable clothes and cars and well, everything." Sydney gestured with her hands.

"Yes, I believe he bought that cute little red thing for Kerri…" Suzanna pondered.

"That little red car belongs to Kerri Blake?" Sydney almost leapt from the chair. She had one of the answers she needed. And it had been so simple – just ask the right person.

Suzanna nodded, surprised that Sydney was so excited by the statement. Sydney questioned her more about Gwen, but Suzanna didn't know much else.

"Do you think you could do me a favor?" Sydney finally asked. "Could you call Claire Burmeister and ask her something for me?"

"How about if I call her in here so no one hears the conversation? We'll put it on speaker phone, and you can ask any additional questions directly." Suzanna pulled out her address book from the top draw and dialed the phone. After thanking her profusely for the judging and show at Showcase, she asked if Sydney Monroe could ask her a few questions she had regarding a comment she made.

"Do you remember making a comment after Gwen Blake's lesson yesterday? It was something about her not being the shy person she pretends to be. What did you mean by that?" Sydney spoke clearly into the speaker.

"Gwen Blake? Oh, yes that young blond girl. I think she has had lots and lots of dance experience, yet she is taking beginner lessons. Could she be from a wealthy family, perhaps? Taken lessons since a young child? She had fabulous technique and knowledge, yet pretends to be a beginner. She even stumbles around when it suites her needs. I think she is not really here to learn dancing. She is here for something else. A man perhaps. She seems to want Mr. Loggerman to think she needs all the help he can give her. She's very needy to go to all that trouble. Is that what you mean?" Claire was crisp and direct.

"I think that is exactly what I mean. Thank you so much," Sydney said with a new life to her voice.

"I would be careful of that one. There is something that is hidden deep down inside," Claire added.

Sydney thanked Claire and Suzanna and left the office. Something during that conversation clicked. She needed to quickly check out something before her lesson. Grabbing her coat, she left by the back door into the parking garage. The little red compact car was still there. Kerri must be teaching a lesson later. But instead of checking the front of the car as one might expect, she came back down the ramp toward the pay booth where Ken was sitting with a toothpick in his mouth reading the paper. She

160

spotted him, stopped and headed back toward the door. Next to the door was parked the Cadillac – Edward's car that was willed to Gwen. It had been sitting there for weeks. Edward had a permanent parking pass that allowed him to park the car year round next to the studio's back door. It was still there. She slowly moved around the car. Edward had parked it so close to the front concrete wall that it was hard to squeeze between the bumper and the wall. She carefully positioned herself so as not to rub or bump the car. Looking down, she saw it. Traces of blood and a dent in the bumper. The Cadillac was built like a tank and unlike one of the newer cars, hitting a deer or person would do little damage. But there were still traces of blood and tissue. Edward had been struck by his own car. Someone had deliberately run him down with the Cadillac and then simply driven around the corner and parked it back where it always sat. No one had bothered to check it. After all, Edward was out in front of the studio when he was killed. But surely Ken had seen someone at least drive out with the car that night. That must be his secret. Maybe he didn't know when Edward was killed, but he had seen him leave with the car and maybe someone else with him. Now just to determine what was so important about this car that he would will it to Gwen

Blake. Surely when he wrote the will he would not have known the car would be an instrument used in his own death.

Sydney quickly entered the studio so as not to arouse notice from Ken who was still absorbed in his paper. She knocked on Suzanna's door once again. Suzanna looked up a bit perturbed this time. It was difficult to have an interruption when working with numbers.

"Sorry," Sydney begged an apology. "But I think we need to call the police immediately. I found the murder weapon."

IX.

It only took a few moments for the detective to get to the studio and into Suzanna's office where Sydney and Suzanna huddled patiently waiting - not wanting to alert anyone else in the studio of the find. It was a miracle that the car had only been mentioned that afternoon in the will and hadn't been moved yet. Then the evidence would have been lost forever – unless a careful Gwen reported something to be amiss with her "new" car. Sydney didn't think that would have happened. They took the detective out the back door to the garage and showed him the front of the car. Immediately he had the car impounded. Casually he walked over to the pay booth to have another chat with Ken. Sydney and Suzanna hovered near by hoping to hear a bit of the conversation.

Ken admitted that Edward Garrett had driven the car out of the ramp that evening. He couldn't quite recall if he had a passenger. "Could be," he mumbled. No, he didn't recall when it came back into its space again. He just hadn't looked behind him to notice. It didn't seem important at the time. Anyone could have parked the car back in its spot and simply walked back up the ramp to the elevator and out another entrance. He didn't recall seeing anyone.

When the conversation was over, Sydney asked both the detective and Suzanna to come back into the studio for a short meeting. When they were securely seated behind closed doors in Suzanna's office, Sydney began to explain some of the strange things she had noticed about Gwen Blake. She repeated the conversation she had overheard from Claire Burmeister after Gwen and Daniel's lesson yesterday and the questions she had just asked in their phone call. She questioned why Edward would will that car to Gwen when it was perfectly logical that Gwen's wealthy father would certainly buy her a car more suited to a young and socially affluent woman.

"I think Edward Garrett was having an affair with Gwen Blake. I think she is the one he was referring to when he mention the Blake fortune to Dennis days before his death. He may have even been having affairs with both the Blake women. Maybe they knew about each other, and maybe they didn't. What if one of them suddenly found out about the other? They both seem to have split second tempers that so far they have been able to control – at least here in the studio. But what if that temper was out of control and one of them killed Edward? They – or she – hit him in the head stunning him so he fell into the road and then ran over him with his own car. They – or she – took the car back to the ramp and parked it again. Then they left in Kerri's car." Sydney laid out her theory carefully.

"The circumstances may point that way," the detective explained. "But we have at this point no hard evidence to back up the theory. We may get some prints from the car. Then again it may be wiped down pretty well. There has been enough time for that to be taken care of quite sufficiently I'm afraid. We need to somehow find more hard evidence to back up this theory because right now that is all it is – a theory."

"Yes, that is why I'm proposing a trap!" Sydney exploded.

"What kind of a trap?" Suzanna sat back into her overstuffed chair and placed her fingers over her mouth as she always did in a time of concern.

"I think that Gwen is falling for Daniel Loggerman," Sydney explained.

"Oh, so she's already moved on to another man," the detective shook his head. "Dangerous for him I'm afraid."

"Kerri already threatened me to stay away from Daniel. I didn't quite understand at the time what she meant, but after watching Gwen preparing for this showcase I can see that she is clearly infatuated with

Daniel. That must be why I received the warning. Anyway, what if I were to ignore that warning? What if I were to appear to get involved with Daniel? Maybe both Kerri and Gwen would show a different side of themselves." Sydney laid out the first part of her plan.

"That is very tricky," the detective warned.

"Yes, and very dangerous," Suzanna kept her hand over her mouth and shook her head slightly.

"We would have to take Daniel into our confidence somewhat so it would appear realistic. And we would need someone else to watch our back. That would have to be someone who is always around the studio and always in and out watching what is going on in other parts of the studio. Someone that wouldn't appear out of place. Antoine for example. He's always out on everyone's lessons and then going back into the teachers' office. He is very observant. We don't want too many people involved in this scheme." Sydney laid out the final part of the plan.

"You and Daniel would both be in great danger if it triggers anything like the reaction Edward received," the detective warned. "I would prefer that we had police around to protect you. I suppose that would be too obvious and out of the question. Unless of course we put a man in as the last appointment of the day – a student – to watch everyone as they leave the building. That might be a possibility. I would think that wise." His brow was knit in thought.

The detective laid out the plan for the undercover police officer and agreed to let Suzanna and Sydney take care of the conversation with Daniel and Antoine. It was decided no one else in the studio would be in on the plan. They couldn't take the chance someone might say the wrong thing to the wrong person and ruin the entire scheme. Later that afternoon, Suzanna pulled Daniel into her office and "had a meeting about his students." She scheduled time with each of the other teachers as well to make it appear normal. Then she met with Antoine to explain the theory and the plan to him.

Suzanna pulled Sydney aside to tell her the plan was in play. But she also revealed that she had been very selective in what she told Daniel. She didn't tell him they suspected Gwen or Kerri. She had been very vague and had cautioned him not to mention anything about this to anyone else. Suzanna said she was hesitant to trust Daniel completely. After all, he had caused some harsh feelings with both Sheila and Megan for some unknown reason. With both of them so affected by his character, she was a bit concerned how trustworthy he was. Sydney nodded agreement and began to prepare for her "new" romance. She started by asking Daniel publicly to stay after studio hours to practice a new routine with her. He had agreed with a sly smile that was sure to make people wonder what they would be practicing.

For the next few days Sydney would always try to be out on the floor somewhere when Daniel had a lesson with Gwen. She would always flirt a little with him before and after the lesson. She began to hang onto Daniel in the back teachers' office between lessons so Kerri was sure to notice. Of course, they would stay after studio hours every evening to dance.

Sydney gained a new student who scheduled every evening in the last appointment slot. His name was listed as "Hans Jansen". It wasn't unusual for a brand new student to do a half hour lesson every day immediately after deciding to take lessons. In fact, it was recommended so the new student could more easily retain the new information presented. She began to recommend that "Hans" attended group lessons also held each evening so he would become more familiar with the other students and staff. "Hans" seemed too normal to be a policeman. He was young, in his early twenties and looked like a typical businessman. He wore his blond curly hair a bit longer, and his athletic build was partially disguised by his stylish basic black suites and conservative shirts and ties. He looked for all the world to be a young executive who needed to learn to dance for an upcoming social event. The other students found him easy to talk with and began to include him in their social plans.

Sydney found "Hans" made her feel safer as she and Daniel began to appear to become more and more of a couple. She appreciated the idea that he was also learning the ins and outs of all the others who were around – both students and staff.

Antoine reported a bit of anxiousness in Kerri's behavior after Sydney left the office area. She was intense in her reaction to the new interest Sydney had for Daniel.

Daniel was easy to feel an attraction for. He was tall and dark haired with a perfect perpetual tan. He could have stepped right out of a fashion magazine page with a natural sense of fashion trends. His smile was infectious and so far he hadn't asked too many questions. That was about to end however.

Daniel and Sydney were huddled at the back table in the ballroom before dance session. After a bit of chit chat, Daniel leaned close and whispered, "So tell me what is really going on here."

"Suzanna already told you. We want to see how the students and other staff members react to a relationship between teachers."

"That isn't what Suzanna told me," Daniel cocked his head to the side and narrowed his eyes and waited for her response. "What's really going on here?"

"OK. We're trying to get a reaction because we think someone in the studio was having a secret affair with Edward Garrett," Sydney didn't think telling part of the plan would hurt. After all, Daniel was being such a good sport about all of this.

"What does that have to do with you and me? And why now?" Daniel persisted leaning back in his chair.

Sydney looked around cautiously and slowly closed the gap between them. "We found the murder weapon," Sydney whispered.

"This is about Edward's murder? And what do you mean you found the weapon?" Daniel's face became less animated. His smile was gone, and he was twisting his usually perfect mouth into a pursed pucker.

"I can't really go into all of that. Not now or here." Sydney looked around with a flit of her eyes trying to change the subject and not dig herself into a deeper hole.

"So what would happen if I mentioned this little tidbit to someone else here in the studio? I don't like feeling like bait. I could change this situation just like that." Daniel was now beginning to look more and more sinister as he glared at Sydney and snapped his finger.

"I hope that isn't a threat, because you are important to this plan." Sydney said with a steady tone in her voice. "Telling someone could make this situation dangerous for both you and me. It might even make you look like a suspect if you are suggesting you might sabotage everything because right now we don't know who or how many were involved in the murder."

Daniel considered this for a moment and with a quick metamorphous became the amiable and smiling person he had been before. This sudden change in personality frightened Sydney. She realized that he certainly had a dark side that wasn't always evident. "Daniel," she began taking his hand once he had calmed down. "I'm sorry to tell you that this is possibly dangerous. We might be trying to flush out a killer. Your help would be greatly appreciated. Especially because no one is really safe in this studio as long as someone here is a possible murderer. I hope you understand that. We felt you could be someone trusted in the matter otherwise we wouldn't have pulled you into this. Do you think you can do your part to just get some kind of reaction from the person - or persons - we are hoping was responsible for the murder of another human being?"

Daniel pondered. Obviously he seemed intrigued by the idea of this being dangerous and considering the enjoyment of play acting a little longer to create a reaction. His eyes seemed to flicker slightly when Sydney mentioned the trust they put in him. He began to feel more in charge of keeping the secret and that seemed to make him feel very powerful. "I like the idea. I'm in. What's next?"

Sydney didn't want to reveal the fact that no one actually did trust him completely – nor even a little bit for that matter. But the feeling that he was going to put his full attention to the plan made her feel a little more secure and confident that it just might work. They began to consider what actions they could take to really make their interest in each other believable to others on the staff and in the studio. Inside, Sydney continued to foster a feeling of distrust that nagged her like a persistent cold symptom. She needed to make sure that "Hans" and Antoine were watching out for her, because she was unsure how far Daniel could be trusted. The other part that bothered her slightly was that he hadn't asked who they suspected. It seemed to simply slip his mind unless he already had some idea who they were trapping. Maybe he already knew.

Later that evening Antoine came out on Sydney's lesson with "Hans" and requested they go over some future dance plans at the end of the lesson which was usual procedure. "Hans" nodded an agreement and the three of them left the floor for Suzanna's office. It would be time for a report on progress.

Once again Suzanna sat in her big overstuffed chair behind the overpowering cherry desk. She seemed somehow to feel more at ease and comfortable in that position than she had when Sydney first visited her about the plan. Her smile and hands folded calmly on the desk top were all indications that she was settling into her new position as a studio owner. No longer did she have that wide eyed startled look as someone who was not in control of the situation. She was clearly "in charge". Her look was more executive with a navy blue blazer and matching skirt accented by a crisp white blouse and colorful scarf tied in a creative knot at her throat.

"Hans" settled into one of the comfortable chairs as did Antoine and Sydney brought in a chair from the waiting area. They closed the door and began to compare notes.

Antoine reported that Kerri Drake was indeed becoming agitated by the relationship of Daniel and Sydney.

"She hasn't confronted me yet," Sydney reported. "But I expect any time to get some kind of verbal threat." Antoine agreed that would be happening soon by all accounts.

"Hans" said he was getting a good feel for the climate at the studio – the staff and the students. He was feeling very accepted by both groups and hoped to be included in some of the student confidences and private conversations in regards to the studio and hopefully Edward's death. He said he had strong feelings that the plot to pull out of hiding a killer was warranted. There definitely was some evidence to suggest the killer was within this group of people associated with the studio. It was just a matter of figuring out who and how many were involved. He wasn't feeling a danger yet, but he suggested Sydney be very careful around Daniel. Daniel seemed to have a hidden agenda.

Sydney reported on the conversation she had with Daniel and agreed with "Hans'" conclusion. There was something that was very much amiss with Daniel. But what that was remained a mystery. They might have to step things up a notch to get a faster reaction. All agreed.

174

The meeting was just long enough for anyone observing to conclude it was a typical student-teacher dance procedure. They all shook hands and left the room satisfied they were on the right track.

Just as they approached the reception desk, the front door opened in a whisk of wind and a tiny woman flew in. "Oh my God, Suzanna!" the woman shrieked in a hoarse voice. "I was out of the country and just heard about Edward. How are you holding up?"

She wrapped her stubby arms around Suzanna, her knit cap falling to the carpet revealing a short blond and red streaked head of hair that stood up like porcupine quills around her heavily made up face. Her arms and hands remained completely covered with a fluffy fake white dotted leopard skin coat and black fuzzy mittens. Upon her tiny feet were the tallest pair of disco shoes imaginable in a glowing red. The base of the shoe was about two inches off the floor with the heel spiking up a good three inches higher. Even with the high shoes, her head came only to Suzanna's shoulders – and Suzanna was a petite woman.

"Milli Mae Carter! How are you?" Suzanna held her out by the arms and stared into her face with a look of relief and relaxed friendship. "Everyone, this is a former teacher Milli Mae Carter. Edward dragged her into this studio and insisted she become a teacher. She was his – well, how shall we put this delicately – Edward's wig stylist."

Milli Mae threw her head back and laughed. "I was really a hair stylist, but for Edward that included the care of his toupees. He was some salesman, I'll have to give you that. Taking me, a hair stylist with a good career and a great income and convincing me that a dance career was what I needed. I loved every minute of it too." She turned again to Suzanna and explained that she had been traveling in Europe and had just returned. Someone she ran into had just happened to mention Edward's death, and she raced to the studio as soon as she heard.

"Scurried" seemed a more appropriate word to Sydney who was completely captivated by this elfin woman. Millie Mae flung her coat onto the couch in the corner and demanded to know everything – "every detail" is how she phrased it. Suzanna ushered her into her office.

Hans, Sydney, and Antoine crowded around the desk scheduling appointments with Morgan and checking out the week on paper. Kerri meandered up smiling and asking Hans how he enjoyed his lessons when Daniel and Gwen came off the floor at the end of their lesson.

"Morgan, when you get a chance, could you check Gwen's lessons for her?" Daniel asked casually and with little emotion as he turned to Sydney. "We better start rehearsal."

His tone was bland and matter of fact. Sydney followed him immediately to the floor, and they began to dance a bit to warm up. Kerri stared after them but said nothing then turned back to Hans to resume their conversation. Gwen seemed absorbed in Morgan checking the week's schedule.

"I don't think this thing is working," Daniel hissed into Sydney's ear.

"Why do you say that?"

"I don't know. I'm not getting any kind of reaction from anyone. No students or staff have said anything about 'us'. Do we need to step it up a notch?" He was a bit agitated as he led her into a cross body lead and under arm turn left.

Suzanna and Millie Mae chattered easily as they left the office and headed toward the desk. Millie Mae was introduced to Gwen and Kerri who seemed to be two towering giants over an Oz sized munchkin. This didn't seem to bother Millie Mae who stuck out her tiny hand to shake, pulled up to her tallest posture and glanced out to the dance floor.

"Whoa! Who's the tall, dark and handsome?" She looked Daniel up and down and whistled.

Everyone including Suzanna and Morgan peered around the corner with shocked looks on their faces. Millie Mae didn't seem to notice instead she pulled her hand back from a stunned Kerri and scurried out to the floor.

"Sorry to interrupt... I'm Millie Mae Carter. And you are?" She ignored Sydney completely as she flashed a smile toward Daniel and extended the back of her hand for an old fashioned kiss from his lips. "You'll have to pardon me. I just got in from Europe and that's how they do it there." Again she flashed a smile.

No one moved. The entire group at the desk stood like statues and watched. Gwen sucked in a breath of air and squeaked out a huff. Kerri's mouth gaped open, and Antoine who knew Millie Mae chuckled under his hand that closed tightly to his mouth.

Finally Hans whispered, "She's not subtle is she." He turned back to Morgan but kept an eye on the floor. Daniel had practically pushed Sydney behind him and was now focusing all of his attentions on this midget of a woman who was tossing questions at him left and right but not waiting for answers.

"My, my, my but aren't you a handsome devil," she finally commented brushing a piece of lint off of her smartly tailored blouse sleeve. Daniel opened his mouth to say something and then simply closed it into a smile.

Well this certainly put a new chink into the plot. What should she do, thought Sydney. Should she butt into the conversation and stake her claim on Daniel Loggerman or simply stand back. What would this new twist do to her carefully planned scheme? She stood helplessly by and watched just like the others as Millie Mae initiated a dance with Daniel. They looked somewhat mismatched but his immaculate posture and her tiny frame had them doing lifts and spins in no time that had everyone gawking in amazement. Millie Mae could twirl faster and tighter than anyone they had ever seen before. Her small size allowed Daniel to pick her up with ease.

X.

Time pasted in slow motion. Soon the show became tedious to watch. Gwen grabbed her coat and headed out the door. Kerri retired to the back teachers' office as had Antoine. Hans followed Gwen out the door and was standing by the parking lot elevator when last seen. Morgan looked a bit perturbed as she plopped pencils into the holder on her desk and snatched her purse to leave.

There were a few flecks of snow starting to fall outside the window that caught the light from the lamp post. The darkness was black and still with no moon.

Daniel and Sydney wandered out to catch the bus pulling their jackets closer around their necks. Daniel commented on the "interesting" night as they waited.

"Interesting? I would say more like 'weird' or maybe even 'now what?' I don't know, but Millie Mae Carter certainly put a new twist on this whole thing. What are we going to do about her?" Sydney huddled in the bus shelter and shook her head.

"Oh, I don't think she ruined anything, do you?" Daniel was looking a bit smug and very pleased with the new admiration and attention from the charming Millie Mae.

"Come on! You can't seriously think that didn't put us back to square one?"

"The only ones to see what happened don't matter anyhow. Antoine, Morgan, Suzanna, Kerri, and Gwen. Who could possibly care what little Miss Carter said and did?" Daniel was clearly not catching on to the plot.

Sydney actually smiled. That meant he didn't really know what the whole point of the trap was. This could be very good or again could be very bad because he wasn't worried about the people she was worried about. It might mean he would let his guard down around the very people he should be most frightened of. Then again she could be wrong.

Suzanna bundled Millie Mae back into her furry coat and suggested they stop into the corner wine bar for a night cap. There were still many things they hadn't talked about other than Edward Garrett's death. Like Millie's trip to Europe, for instance. And Suzanna hadn't yet mentioned that she was the owner of the studio. Maybe she could convince Millie Mae to return to teaching. She could always use another teacher who was already trained. A trained ballroom teacher was like a gold mine to a dance studio owner.

The bar was quiet and mellow with only a few scattered patrons as they took their seats on the high stools back in the corner by the window. Millie Mae hopped up onto hers like a butterfly to a flower. The snow was now flying a little more, and the scene was serene and calming. They sipped their wine and ordered a plate of hors devours. The Europe stories were both funny and very Millie Mae. She was one who never had an experience that could be considered "normal". There was always something about any story from Millie Mae that was slightly off. They laughed at her attempts at sightseeing that went terribly wrong and at her trials with the European driving system. It was one of the few times since Edward's death that Suzanna laughed. The wine made her head spin a bit, and she was feeling very relaxed. When it was time to leave, Suzanna thought about taking a taxi. But the snow and weather were so peaceful that they both decided to take the late bus. Millie was living at her sister's house off of Lake Street, but begged to come back to Suzanna's apartment and crash on her couch for the night. It was late after all and would give them added chance to talk.

They bundled up and stepped outside. The street was quiet and empty with a light frost coating the sidewalk. The bar was only a block from the bus stop to the right and a block from the studio on the left. Still chatting away, they began to slowly teeter toward the bus stop. Millie Mae's shoes were not made for snow, and Suzanna held tightly to her arm so she wouldn't slip on the accumulating snow. Millie Mae was giggling as she sloshed back and forth on the side walk trying desperately to keep her balance.

Suddenly a darkness loomed over them, and Suzanna turned just in time to see a shadow of a figure holding a bat above their heads. Just as Suzanna's reflexes hunched to withstand the impact from the club, it was quickly yanked backwards causing the dark figure to stumble and crash to the ground. Millie Mae leaned into Suzanna, and they struggled to stay on their feet as the mugger with the bat was overpowered. With a sudden kick, the figure on the ground let go of the bat and sliding sideways, stood to run minus the weapon. At that moment a car careened around the corner and in a swoop picked up the figure, screeched loudly away with the headlights picking up the fragments of swirling snow. Just as quickly it was gone.

Suzanna stood shaking as Hans appeared from the darkness quickly fishing his phone from his belt and calling in a request to the dispatcher to have patrols on the lookout for a small red car.

"Are you all right?" Hans held Suzanna's arm as she clung to Millie Mae. Millie Mae was completely stunned. She didn't know what had happened. She seemed unaware that she had just experienced a life threatening moment.

"Who was that?" Suzanna's calm and peaceful mood was now shaken. She stammered a bit as she stared into Hans' face.

"I felt that something was going to happen tonight. It was very evident that Millie Mae had stirred up some underlying feelings by paying such close attention to Daniel. And I decided to follow her this evening just in case. I guess that was a wise instinct." Hans opened his coat to reveal his holster and the beeping police phone. He picked up the call and mumbled something back.

"A patrol car spotted the car and is following, but I'm afraid there is going to be some trouble. The ladies, Gwen and Kerri Blake are not about to stop at this point and there seems to be a chase situation. We'll have to wait for a report." Hans tucked the phone back into his belt. "This weather won't help." He looked around into the sky frowning at the faster falling snow flakes.

"So it was Kerri and Gwen. Did you see which one was doing the swinging?" Suzanna felt a bit faint.

"No. They both have the same tall build, and the one carrying the bat was covered with a black coat and hood. They were certainly both involved but I can't say for sure which one is the murderer and which was driving the car," he reported.

"Murderer? What is this about?" Millie Mae was now beginning to breathe harder. She was curled tightly into Suzanna's arms. There would be much more to talk about this evening just as Suzanna had predicted, but it wouldn't be about fun and games in Europe. It had now opened up a much more serious topic.

XI.

"I think Sydney Monroe's theory was right on. One of them followed Edward Garrett from the studio, struck him in the head with a bat or club, then they both ran over him with Edward's car before taking it back to the parking ramp and leaving it to sit undisturbed." Hans was describing the scene to the dance studio staff seated at the glass tables in the ballroom. "Patrol cars pursued Kerri Blake's car early this morning and with the snow and slippery conditions, her car slammed into an underpass. Gwen Blake was killed instantly. Kerri Blake was thrown free and now is in the hospital with two broken legs and multiple other injuries. We are at this point unsure which of the two was driving and who was the passenger. We will continue to investigate the circumstances of the accident, but we do know at this point that we have solved Edward Garrett's murder."

no good.

"I guess we were lucky," Daniel leaned over toward Sydney. "I guess we were lucky they didn't actually believe our little charade."

"Just what do you mean by that?" Sydney blurted out with a scowl on her face.

"If they had, they would have come after us, wouldn't they?" Daniel asked.

Sydney settled back into her chair content that she had come up with some of the key evidence and the plan that finally had led to the capture of the murderer – dead or not. "I guess thinking is my strength and not acting."

XII.

In the end, it had all worked out. Hans Jensen went back to being a policeman and not a dance student although he stopped in for a group class occasionally. The students even with their network for gossip, never realized that he was a cop Suzanna settled into her new studio and even became comfortable in Edward's office. The primitive art slowly disappeared as the staff claimed their bequeaths from Edward. Portraits and paintings of dancers began to grace the walls and bring a new cheery lightness to the once dark office.

Although Suzanna wanted Millie Mae to come back to teach in the studio, Millie and Daniel decided to sign on as a dance team, entertaining guests for a cruise line. Their tall and short partnership had intrigued the person hiring new talent for the shows. Millie Mae eventually began to grow tired and dislike Daniel intensely just as Megan and Sheila had. She could never quite put her finger on the reason, but their partnership was a strain for both of them it seemed. Daniel quickly grew just as tired of Millie Mae and her energetic personality. When Milli found out Daniel had AIDS, it was an excuse to get off the ship, come back to the studio and once again teach for Suzanna. Daniel died shortly after and not surprisingly there were few tears shed at his funeral.

With Daniel gone and no new teacher willing to move into the duplex, Megan needed to make some decisions as well. Antoine and Megan decided to move out to Las Vegas when a position for manager in one of the dance studios became available. That lasted for about a year before Antoine signed on with a Las Vegas hotel dance troupe. He danced in Las Vegas for another year then accepted a dance position with the new troupe formed when the chain opened a hotel in Paris. Megan came back home also working for Suzanna – this time in the Counselor position abandoned by Antoine.

Kerri Blake slowly recovered from her injuries and maintained her innocence in the murder of Edward Garrett and the attempt on Millie Mae Carter's life. She was acquitted of charges claiming it was Gwen Blake who was the murderer. With Gwen dead, there was no concrete evidence tying Kerri to any of the events directly. She moved on to New York and became a top magazine model.

Amanda Garrett works in fashion as she has her entire life. She has begun to add choreographer to her long line of career titles and does put together some amazing fashion extravaganzas for the "elite" fashion industry in

Minneapolis. She remains in her humble little apartment in Suzanna's four-plex and has not attempted to become involved in another serious relationship. It seems after a marriage to Edward Garrett, no one else compares. Life with anyone else feels...well, just plain dull. Or maybe she has a deep seated fear of trusting anyone again.

Sydney Monroe is still teaching and dancing and giving opinions when something puzzling pops up. That of course happens all the time in the world of dance. That of course happens all the time.

Tango Basic:

Man's part: Forward on the left foot (count Slow), Forward on the right foot (count Slow), Forward on the left foot (count Quick), Side to the right with the right foot (count Quick), Close left foot to right with no weight on the left foot (count Slow).

Woman's part: Back on the right foot (count Slow), Back on the left foot (count Slow), Back on the right foot (count Quick), Side to the left with the left foot (count Quick), Close the right foot to the left with no weight on the right foot (count Slow).

www.ingramcontent.com/pod-product-compliance
Lightning Source LLC
Chambersburg PA
CBHW061204170626
46809CB00003B/1234